DARYL LOVE

Ride or Die

This novel is entirely a work of fiction. The names, characters and incidents portrayed in it are the work of the author's imagination. Any resemblance to actual persons, living or dead, events or localities is entirely coincidental.

First edition

Cover art by Chemieka Amuzu
Editing by Chemieka Amuzu

This book was professionally typeset on Reedsy.
Find out more at reedsy.com

I dedicate this to my parents. Though you're no longer here, your spirit dwells within me. You raised a great man—a leader, a visionary. To those who believed in me when I was discouraged, thank you. To my Lord and Savior—I understood the assignment. To everyone who contributed to my legacy—I won't let you down. And to the one who kept me grounded through it all... I give high dedication to ME.
Thank you.
From Rich DOG Entertainment

Contents

Prologue

"**FREEZE!** Don't move!

I mean it! Don't... move..."

The detective's voice sliced through the night like a box-cutter—sharp, urgent, shaking with adrenaline. Gun drawn. Arms stiff. Steps slow but steady. The suspect twisted his head—just enough to peek.

That's all he needed.

He saw it: Holzendorf was too far back. No clean shot. No backup in reach.

So he did what any real one would do with death breathing down his neck—He ran.

"He's on the run!"

a voice screamed through the walkie.

"He's in the backyard—heading for the fence!"The night exploded.

"He cleared the fence! **I SEE HIM!** I want two cruisers on every corner, ten-block radius! This son of a bitch is not getting away!"

Sirens wailed from all angles. Red and blue lights bounced off brick. Rubber screeched. Helicopter blades chopped overhead, wind slashing trees apart. Holzendorf raised his weapon again—sight locked on the figure darting through the alley.

"**I SAID FREEZE!**"

He thought he had me. Thought it was lights out right there.

But let me clear it up for you—That dude they chasin'? The one runnin' like the whole city just caught fire?
Yeah, that's me.
Name's Tiger.
How I got into this mess—or how I got out—is a whole damn saga.
You ready for it?
'Cause that cop behind me? That's Detective Holzendorf. The city's most stubborn bloodhound. And for years, I been the scent he can't shake.

Now picture this: half the department on my ass, helicopters lighting up rooftops, every block boxed in like a game of Tetris.
It looks like checkmate.
But nah.
This ain't that kinda story.
You wanna know how I ended up in
this hellified situation?
Good.
Because I'm about to take you on a ride where survival ain't a choice—
It's ride or die.

1

Keys, Codes, and Consequences

"Tiger! Get up," Cookie stated as she nudged Tiger vigorously. "Get up, baby. Your phone is getting on my nerves."

Still no response. Tiger moaned and rolled over. He had a long night the night before and got home late. She held the phone over his head so he could hear the ringing.

"You want me to answer it? It's probably one of your lil' girlfriends calling back to back," she stated sarcastically as she looked at the phone.

No name popped up, just a number. Tiger never programmed names in his phone—for federal reasons. Regardless of what she said, he knew she prowled through his phone. What self-respected woman wouldn't?

"Hello," Cookie stated, pretending to answer his phone.

Tiger immediately jumped up as if he was having a bad dream. He quickly reached for his phone.

"Girl, you play too much," he stated as he sat up and put his ear to the phone.

Cookie glanced with a suspicous look
on her face.

"Mm-hmm," she huffed. "Let me find out you playing around, ima cut ya lil peepee off."

Cookie loved Tiger with all she had, but she had her limits. There was countless he say/she say, but nothing solid.

"**WHAT THE HELL YOU MEAN?**" Tiger screamed through the phone as he lunged up out the bed. Cookie watched him charge into the bathroom and slam the door. She sat for a moment, about to eavesdrop, when Tiger flung the door open again.

"**WHO ALL WAS THERE?**" he yelled, grabbing his pants, shoes, and shirt. "**DON'T MOVE! I'MA BE RIGHT THERE!**"

He hung up and clenched the phone like he was choking somebody. Then he started frantically searching the room.

"What happened?" Cookie asked, sitting up in bed, wearing the silk white nighty Tiger
loved so much.

"Where are my keys?" Tiger snapped,
ignoring her question.

"What happened?" she asked again, watching him sling items off the dresser.

"**WHERE ARE MY DAMN KEYS?**" Tiger barked, voice harder.

Cookie stood up on the bed and walked toward him. "Where you think you going?
You just got home."

Cookie stood 5'5", pecan tan complexion, with breasts and ass to die for. She had on his favorite piece—no bra, no panties. Tiger noticed. He wanted to slam her on the floor and take her right there, but he had bigger shit to handle.

"I gotta make a run," he said calmly.
"I'mma be right back."

4

"You just got home not too long ago,"
she pleaded.
"I'm not about to go back and forth with you. Now, have you
seen my damn keys or not?"
She walked to the dresser, opened the top drawer, and pulled
them out.
"Here," she huffed, shoving them into his chest and turning
away. Tiger grabbed her,
pulling her close.

"Don't act like that," he said, voice low. "Just gotta handle
something real quick."
"You always gotta handle something,"
she said, pulling away.
Tiger wanted to comfort her, but what he had to handle came
first.
Cookie knew the pattern. Whine a little, get in bed with her back
turned, pull the covers to her shoulder—Tiger would slide in,
apologize, and it'd be all good. But not today.
"I said I'll be back. Dang," Tiger huffed, heading to the door.
"You just gotta trust me."
He shut it behind him.
Cookie stood still, heart thudding. She knew it was bad. Eyes
closed, she whispered, "God, please cover him."

***

Tiger hurried across town. He was pissed, and someone was
about to feel it. When he got on Myrtle Ave., he slowed down a
bit. That was an area known to be swarmed with cops.
Tiger seemed to feel he was partly
responsible for that. He and his crew had spots all through
Jacksonville.

He was partly responsible for supplying at least 80% of the coke within Duval, Nassau, and Clay County. The F.E.D.S. had been trying to plant a case on Tiger for some time now, but he always seemed to be two steps ahead. Turning down 16th & Myrtle, toward the dead end, the street looked more quiet than normal.

But it was 3 A.M. In this particular area, Tiger appointed a captain—Ace—and two lieutenants: Dred and Charles. Parking in front of the apartment, Tiger noticed a black Mercedes CLK, which belonged to Ace, a black Hummer, which was Charles's, a candy red Cadillac CTS, which was Dred's, and two Cadillac DeVilles—which meant there were more people on payroll.

Tiger got out of his Escalade and slowly walked around the apartment. All the cameras were in place—no sign of forced entry through the front or back doors, nor the windows. Tiger knew they could see him outside, even when he turned on the street.

"Somebody better make some sense of this," Tiger mumbled to himself.

He walked up on the porch, about to reach for the door, when an unfamiliar face greeted him. He knew it had to be one of the new jits.

"Wuzup, Tiger?" the jit said.

Tiger was so upset, he brushed past him, looking for Ace. Ace and Dred were going back and forth about the situation that happened just hours ago. Charles was listening in, but not commenting.

The jit that answered the door walked over and sat by the other jit on the couch, who was rolling up some weed. Tiger took a last-minute surveillance around the apartment. There were three guns by the table, and he was sure Ace or Dred had one on them.

"WHO THE FUCK ARE Y'ALL?" Tiger demanded, glancing at the jits.

Before they could speak, Charles cut in. "Oh, this umm... Breezy and Charles." They both nodded their heads in a 'wuzup' motion.

Tiger turned his attention toward Ace. "So what the hell happened? And it better be good."

Ace glanced down, shaking his head. He too couldn't explain what happened.

"Who the hell was it?" Tiger asked, but got no response.

"How the **FUCK** did they get in?"

Still no response.

"Somebody better tell me something before I start wetting shit up in here."

Tiger wasn't known to be the violent type. But Tupac said it best: *I ain't no killa, but don't push me.* Everyone was still afraid to answer.

"Alright... I see!" Tiger huffed, glancing around the room at all the nervous, confused faces. "How many was it?"

"**THREE**," they all said in unison.

Tiger pondered for a moment, then spoke. "So y'all telling me, three dudes came up in my spot—" He paused for a moment, remembering: *no forced entry.* "How did they get in?"

Ace, Dred, nor Charles felt safe about answering that. After a brief moment of silence, Charles—the jit—blurted out, "Mr. Tiger, the shit happened so crazy—."

Tiger glanced over his shoulder at the jit speaking.

"Jit, this don't concern you. You may wanna just sit yo ass down somewhere and keep quiet."

7

He quickly sat down and lit up the blunt he'd just finished rolling.

"PUT THAT SHIT OUT!" Tiger yelled.

"Who is this dude?" Tiger asked sarcastically, turning his attention back to Ace.

"Somebody better tell me what happened before shit gets ugly."

Ace was about to speak when Tiger cut him off. "Before you speak—explain how they got in, what happened, and how the **FUCK** they got away wit three hunnit stacks and five bricks—and not one damn shot was fired."

No one knew the answer. Not one that would make any sense.

"I can explain," Charles, the jit, blurted out.

Tiger took a deep breath before snapping.

"Jit, you got one more time to make yo presence known. For all I know, this was a setup—and **ALL** y'all niggas guilty."

"Tiger, it wasn't like that," Ace cut in.

"THEN WHAT WAS IT LIKE?" Tiger snapped. **"MY MONEY GONE! MY DOPE GONE! NO FORCED ENTRY! GUNS EVERY FUCKIN' WHERE!** Yet, no bullet holes in the wall, no blood, no bodies on the ground, and ain't none of y'all niggas tied up. Seems fuckin' incredible to me... or is it just a strange coincidence?"

Tiger pulled out his pistol, knowing it would spark fear.

"Tell me suttin', Ace."

Ace thought for a moment, then spoke.

"They came in—"

"Stop right there!" Tiger cut in.

"Y'all **LET** them in."

"Whatever, T—"

"Ain't no damn whatever! That's what happened, right?" Tiger snapped angrily.

"I guess," Ace humbly stated.

"You guess, huh? You guess?"

Tiger was extremely pissed at this point. He clutched his pistol even harder.

"Y'all let 'em in, y'all gave 'em my shit,
and they left."

"That's not what happened, T," Dred spoke, leaning in the corner.

"Y'all don't seem to know what happened. But what I do know is that y'all—" he pointed his pistol at everyone in the room— "every one of y'all owe me five bricks and three hunnit stacks. **OR GET MY SHIT BACK.**"

No one answered.

"And I want the heads of everyone involved."

Everyone shook their heads, thinking they got off easy, but Tiger was far from done.

"This shit still seems shady..." He looked over at Ace. "And you were in charge?"

"Tiger, I'm tellin' ya, homie... shit was crazy," Ace responded quickly.

"Crazy, huh?" Tiger stated, walking closer.

"He right, Tiger," Charles cut in.

"Shit seemed unreal."

"What's unreal is that I'm five keys and three hunnit stacks in the hole." He began mean-mugging Ace and lightly clenching his pistol "I'mma handle it," Ace stated humbly.

"You gonna handle it, huh?" Tiger asked sarcastically, shaking his head. "Nah, you've done enough." He took a deep breath. "You not capable of runnin' my shit."

Ace was about to plead his side when—**POW!** Tiger put a bullet

9

through Ace's right eye. Everyone in the apartment jumped back in horror as Ace's body dropped. When Tiger turned to face everyone else, you could've heard a mosquito fart with the silence.

"I want my money. And everyone involved—dead."

He pointed his pistol down at Ace. "Or this will be y'all." He slowly walked toward the door. Before he reached it, he spoke—without glancing back: "Dred. You in charge now."

Dred nodded in agreement. "Handle this.

Or I'll be back."

He walked out, and everyone finally began to breathe again.

"FUUUUCK!" Breezy stated.

"Tiger be wildin' out."

"This ain't even like him," Charles defended."You think he serious?" Charles' lil' jit asked."Serious about what?" Dred said, as he and Charles began getting Ace up to figure out what to do with his body.

"About killin' us."

There was a deafening pause. Dred bent down, grabbed Ace's body by the arms, and started dragging. He stopped at the door, looked back—expression cold.

"Y'all don't get it... That was his first cousin."

2

No Turning Back

"Now that's what you call a sweet lick," Spank said excitedly.

"I told ya," Taz confirmed, still counting everything they had grabbed.

"How much is in there?" Champ asked, glancing at Taz through the rearview.

Taz had already counted over a hundred thousand and still had bundles left. "Prolly 'bout two or three hunnit stacks."

"Heeeell fuck yeeah!" Champ shouted, bouncing around in his seat.

Taz kept digging through the bag and spotted a rectangular-shaped package. I know this ain't what I think it is, he mumbled. His eyes widened as he pulled it out.

"WHAAAT! YEEEAH!"

They were so hyped, none of them noticed the gas light beeping low.

"Let's get to the spot and count this cash."

"And that work," Spank added.

"How many in there?" he asked,
eyeing the bricks.

Taz knew it was five, but greed kicked in.

"It's three," he said,

knowing they wouldn't question it.

"What you doin' wit yo cash, Spank?" Champ asked, grinning like he had

a Kool-Aid sponsorship.

Spank paused, then smirked. "A couple stacks, I'm ballin' at the Silver Foxx. A couple more bands at Mascara. A couple at Bottoms Up.

A couple at—"

"Whoa, whoa, whoa," Champ cut in. "You blowin' yo flow on strippers?"

"Nah! Not all of it. Just a couple bands," he defended. "I gotta let the ladies know

I'm that dude."

"Yeah, that dumb dude," Taz cut in, laughing. "What you gonna do, big money?"

Spank asked Taz.

"I know what I'mma do," Champ jumped in, turning in his seat. "I'mma buy me a vert and trick that bitch out. Sit it on some eights. Nah, some thirties... yeah, thirties."

Champ was deep in thought until

Taz blurted, "That's it?"

"Nah! I'mma buy me a pound of the most sticky-ickiest shit I can find, and smoke

til' I'm paralyzed."

"YEEEAH!" Champ grinned.

"Y'all both idiots," Taz snapped.

"And what you plan on doing wit yours?"

Spank asked. "Donate it to the homeless?"

"Nah, he gonna turn it in to the police,"

Champ laughed.

"I'mma take over the South Side!

That's what I'mma do," Taz said.

"Wit one kilo?" Champ asked, sarcastic.

"You the next Frank Lucas?"

"Nah, nah, Champ. He the next Big Meech."

They cracked up, breaking into Young Jeezy's *You think you ballin' cause you got a block.*

"Just get to the spot," Taz said. "I can show ya betta than I can tell ya."

***

Driving down University Blvd. toward Ft. Caroline Arms Apartments, the car

started sputtering.

"What's wrong wit dis raggedy-ass car?"

Taz asked.

"I don't know," Spank said, while pumping

the gas pedal.

Champ leaned over to check the dash.

"You outta gas, genius."

"It's a Hess station up on the left,"

Champ added. "See if you can cruise all the way there "Cause I ain't pushin'," Taz said.

Pullin' up to the pump, Champ and Spank headed into the store. Taz stayed in the car, guarding the money.

"What pump we at?"

Spank asked, glancing back.

"Umm, four," Taz said, snappin' out his trance.

This was the perfect time to duck off those other two kilos. He popped the trunk and started rummaging—didn't even see the cop car pull up behind him.

***

"Grab me a Arizona," Spank asked Champ, heading into the bathroom.

"Aahite," he responded.

As Champ walked back to the cooler,
the officer walked in.

"We got fresh coffee and donuts out, Phil," the clerk said to the cop.

"Is that right?" the officer responded with a smile. "Well let me help myself before sunrise."

As he walked down the aisle near the bathroom toward the donuts, he and Spank missed each other by just a few seconds.

"Ya got er'thing?" Spank asked as they
headed to the counter.

"Yeah, I'm good. I'm ready to get back
to the spot."

"Two Arizona's and a Gatorade," the clerk stated, scanning the items. "Three-fifty."

Spank handed him a twenty. "Put the rest on pump—" He looked outside to verify the pump and froze. The cop car was parked behind them.

Champ noticed his frozen look and glanced out to see what was up.

"Oh shit! Oh shit! Oh shit!"
he said, breathing heavy.

"What pump, sir?" the clerk asked.

Champ saw the cop wasn't in the car—but he couldn't see Taz either. He turned, scanning the store, and stood face to face with the officer.

He nudged Spank as he turned around, grabbing his attention. Spank looked back and immediately turned toward the cashier.

"The pump, sir?" the cashier asked again.

"Is that yall on pump four?"

Every time they looked outside, all they saw was the cruiser.

"Y-y-yeah," Spank mumbled.

"Okay. Sixteen-fifty on pump four."

They ran out the store like a bat outta hell.

"Youngsters," the cop said as he stepped up to the counter. "These donuts not fresh. These yesterday donuts," he joked, and both he
and the clerk laughed.

They glanced out the window just in time to see Taz, Spank, and Champ speeding off.

"It's too early in the morning to be chasing these lil' knuckle-heads," the cop muttered,
shaking his head.

The cashier glanced at the gas meter and laughed. "Guess they were in a rush—left without pumpin they gas."

"They'll be back," the cop said,
handing over ten dollars.

After a beat, Officer Phil squinted, something about the whole thing not sitting right. He grabbed his donut and coffee and hustled out the door.

"PHIL, YO CHANGE!"
the cashier called after him.

"I'll swing back through later!" Officer Phil shouted, sliding into his cruiser and peeling off in the direction the boys had gone.

***

"Boy, I was nervous than a mug," Champ said, now sitting in the back.

"You think you were scared?" Taz added. "Imagine not paying attention, then you look up and **BAM**! Cop right there."

"That's pretty much what happened,"
Spank cut in.

As they passed University and Merrill Road, the gas warning chimed again, snapping everyone's attention.

"You didn't pump the gas, Taz?"
Champ asked, nervous.

"ME?" he shot back. "Y'all the ones came out the store and just jumped in the car."

"'Cause we assumed you had already pumped the gas," Spank added.

"Man, I saw the cop behind us—car full of dope and money—so all I thought about was gettin' outta there."

"Well, it's over and done wit now. Just stop at the next station and fill up," Spank replied.

"If we make it," Champ muttered.

"Oh, we gonna make it," Taz huffed.

But when Taz glanced in the rearview, his heart dropped. He whipped around to confirm. He was right.

"I SEE POLICE LIGHTS COMING UP THE STREET!" Taz yelled.

Both Champ and Spank looked back fast.

"Shit! Shit! Shit!" Champ panicked. "This can't be happening."

"Man, chill out," Taz snapped, trying to keep it cool. "They too far back to know if they
after us or not."

"It's prolly that same cracka we saw at the gas station," Champ said, still panicked.

"FLOOR IT!" Spank barked.

Taz stomped the pedal—but the car sputtered. **"FUUUCK!"**

Taz roared, punching the steering wheel. "What's wrong?" Champ asked.

"Gas too low."

"He comin' up fast," Spank said.

"Switch lanes," Champ added. "Maybe he'll keep going. He might don't want us."

Taz switched lanes. The cop did too. Seconds later, the cruiser was riding their bumper.

"What to do?" Champ asked, jittery.

"Let's jump out."

"Hell nah," Spank snapped. "This my sista car. They'll go straight to her house and

she'll give 'em our info."

"We ain't jumpin' out,"

Taz said calmly, eyes locked on the mirror.

"We betta decide suttin quick, before he call backup—and we'll be really screwed,"

Champ added.

"So what's the plan?" Spank asked.

"We'll pull over," Taz said, firm.

"HELL NAH!" Champ cut in. "Dumb plan!

Very, very dumb plan."

But Taz was already slowing up, easing toward the shoulder. They all clicked in their seatbelts, trying to look halfway presentable. "Driver! Cut the car off and put your hands out the window," the officer commanded

through the intercom.

"Don't do it!" Champ pleaded.

"It's not too late to run."

Taz paused, thinking.

"It's three of us and one of him," Champ pushed. "What about Spank's sista?"

"Fuck that!" Champ snapped. "We cross that bridge when we get there!"

Spank started getting nervous too. "We'll just tell her her car was stolen.

Have her call it in or something."

Taz shook his head—no—and slowly placed his hands out the window. The cop stepped out of his cruiser, hand resting on his pistol,

moving in slow.

"I got this," Taz said, steady.

"Let's see what he got."

"License, registration, and proof

of insurance, please."

Champ reached in the glove box and passed Taz the papers.

"How are you this morning, officer?" Taz asked as he handed over the info.

"Is this your vehicle?" the cop asked, glancing

at the documents.

"No sir—"

"It's my sister's car, sir," Spank cut in

from the back.

The officer paused.

"Do you mind me askin' what you pulled me over for?" Taz asked.

"Y'all sit tight for a moment."

He took the papers and headed back to his car. "Suttin ain't right," Champ said, voice low. "I got a bad feelin' about this."

"We ain't do nuttin. If we sit tight and act cool, he gotta keep it

movin',” Taz said,
watching the mirror.
“Chill, chill. Here he come.”

Officer Phil returned to the window,
holding the paperwork.
“You mind steppin' out of the vehicle, sir?” “Don't do it,”
Champ whispered.
“What's wrong, officer?” Taz asked, hesitant. “Are you aware
your license is suspended?”
“Oh Lord. Here we go wit this shit,”
Spank groaned.
“I told ya! I...told ya,” Champ cut in as
Taz stepped out.
“I'm fenta run.”
“Don't move,” Spank said. “I have an idea.”

He looked out the window and spotted Taz by the rear bumper.
Slipping out the door, gun in hand, he moved beside him. Officer
Phil was still in his cruiser, distracted.
“What you think he doin'?” Spank whispered. “Prolly callin'
backup,” Taz said.
“What ya thinkin'?”
“Don't know,” Taz replied. “Would bounce, but he got my info.
I just know I'm not goin' to jail tonight.”
“I'm waaaay ahead of ya.”

Spank moved from around Taz and headed toward Officer
Phil's car. Phil immediately jumped out with his hand on his
pistol.
“Get back in the car, sir!” Officer Phil demanded. “I wanna ask a
question,” Spank pleaded,
trying to get closer.
“Sir, get back in the car.

I'm not gonna say it again."
Spank paused for a moment,
debating—yes or no.
"Come on back, Spank," Taz tried to plead.

Spank looked over his shoulder at Taz and mumbled, "I'm not going to jail tonight."
Before he could think twice, he revealed the gun behind his back and let off several shots toward Officer Phil. Phil tried to pull his piece,
but was riddled with bullets.
"Oh shit! Oh fuck! Oh shit!" Champ shouted, hearing the shots and seeing the cop go down. "WHAT THE FUCK!" he screamed. "You shot a cop!"
Spank walked over.
The officer was still barely alive.
"Let's go!" Taz pleaded.
"He still alive!" Spank said nervously,
gun still pointed.
"You can't kill a cop!" Champ tried to negotiate. He saw the tension in Spank's face,
dude was serious.
"Think about this, Spank. Once you do this… there's no turning back."
   Spank's palm started sweating. His gun was getting heavier by the second. Officer Phil lay sprawled out, barely holding on, as Spank faced a life-changing decision. Phil knew this was it. He took one last breath…
"I don't plan on turnin' back…"
   POW.

3

Cold as Ice

Tiger pulled up at his house—aggravated, tired, upset, and thinking, *What the hell am I gonna tell my aunt?* He had overreacted, and he couldn't take it back.

"What the fuck was I thinking?" he stated, punching the steering wheel, accidentally alerting the horn. He saw his bedroom light turn on, and Cookie looking through the blinds.

"Here we go with this shit," he mumbled to himself as he got out and headed to the house. He had been so distracted that he forgot he put his phone on silent. He was supposed to meet Heavy and Pie Yay to holla at the connect.

***

"He answered yet?" Pie asked Heavy, as he attempted to call Tiger.

"Where this nigga at, man?" Pie continued. "Maybe he runnin' late," Heavy stated, trying to make an excuse.

"Man, I feel like a sittin' duck out here in the middle of nowhere with this cash on us like this," Pie pleaded, looking back and forth for anyone to walk or drive up.

"You think he called the connect?" Pie asked. "Yeah! I guess... I know he called a couple days ago," Heavy added.

"Maybe he cancelled til—"

Before Pie Yay could get out his statement, Heavy spotted a set of headlights
in the rearview.

"Who is that?" Pie asked. Heavy squinted his eyes to try to look.

"I don't know. You got yo pistol?"

Pie Yay pulled his trusted 9mm from inside his pants. "Time to ride or die!"

Before Heavy could make any moves, he saw two dudes in dark suits step out the
front of a Suburban.

"Who the hell?" Heavy wondered.

"Dude!" Pie spoke, surprised.

"That's the connect!"

"You sure?" Heavy asked, gripping his pistol.

His answer was confirmed when a U-Haul pulled up with the logo:

Cold as Ice, Ice Industries.

"Yeah, I'm sure," he stated with a smile.

"Didn't he say his name was Ice?"

Heavy nodded.

"Then it's on, baby!

The man of the hour has arrived."

The two guys wearing the suits walked toward Heavy's Yukon. After opening their doors, both Heavy and Pie were instructed to proceed to the back of the truck.

"Wussup big homie?" Heavy spoke, trying to release the tension, but got no response.

"Wait right there!" one of the guards demanded. Each guard

patted Heavy and Pie down, finding Pie's 9mm and Heavy's .40 caliber.

"Be careful with that," Pie huffed, pointing at his pistol. "That's my baby."

When they were cleared of the weapons check, one of the guards spoke into an earpiece, mentioning it was all clear. Suddenly, the back door of the Escalade the guards pulled up in opened. The first thing Heavy and Pie noticed was a shoe. A size 14 gator-skin Stacy Adams, with diamond-encrusted highlights.

Seconds later, out stepped Ice.

It was very easy to see where he got the name Ice from. It was four in the morning, yet it looked as if a spotlight was shining directly on him. He wore a diamond-embedded, Jay-Z edition Presidential Cartier watch. A two-inch thick, indigo-blue and clear diamond bracelet. His earring was a five-karat indigo-blue, quarter-inch thick, cube-shaped special edition. Three platinum and diamond finger rings. Even his buttons and cuff links were diamond.

"This nigga shining," Pie Yay envied.

"Move forward," one of the guards stated to Heavy and Pie.

They were directed to walk toward the U-Haul, where they stood face to face with Ice. "Where's Tiger?" he stated in a deep, stern voice. "I don't know, Mr. Ice! We've been callin' him all morning," Pie spoke.

"Gentlemen, let's keep it casual here. Mr. Ice is my father," he stated with a smile, as one of the guards lit the cigar he placed in his mouth. He took a few puffs, blew out a slow, cool breeze of smoke and spoke, "It's just Ice."

Heavy and Pie both nodded in agreement. Ice knew they had to be speaking the truth, because he'd called Tiger several times himself

and got no answer.

"Heavy! Right?" He pointed at Heavy—which wasn't hard to figure out, being that he was nearly 300 pounds, with a head full of dreads and a pudgy stomach. And Pie was 180 pounds with a low cut.

"How'd ya guess?" they both laughed.

"Humor. I like that,"

Ice stated, taking another puff. "It eases the sometimes tension of business."

He walked over to the back of the U-Haul. "Speaking of business..." He lifted the U-Haul door. Inside were two armed guards carrying semi-automatic assault rifles.

"This was a fuckin' setup!" Pie snapped, looking into an empty U-Haul. He held his hands in the air, as if submitting.

"Put your hands down, youngster. You look ridiculous," Ice said, stepping inside the seemingly empty U-Haul. "You didn't think I'd have a transport vehicle with drugs all out in the open, did ya?"

He walked by Heavy and nudged him.

"You see that red button that says Push In Case of Emergency?"

Heavy nodded, still hesitant.

"Push it."

Heavy slowly walked over to the button

and looked back at Ice to

double-check confirmation.

With a heavy laugh, Ice stated, "It ain't gonna bite ya, homie. It's safe."

Heavy pushed the button, and the U-Haul began to transform. The metal door up front

became a sliding door.

It separated, revealing six 55-gallon drums.

"Viola," Ice spoke.

"Hot diggity dog damn," Pie stated, staring at the drums, knowing what was in them. Tiger had brought several packages in, packaged the same way.

Both Heavy and Pie ran up to the drums and immediately opened them. The smell almost knocked them off their feet. Each drum held fifty kilos inside.

"Now this Wassup," Pie Yay confirmed, with a money-hungry grin on his face.

"Now. It's time for y'all end of the deal,"
Ice cut in.

Heavy and Pie glanced at each other, confused. "My money," Ice reminded.

"Oh! Yeah! Yo money."

Heavy and Pie both headed to the truck to grab the cash.

"You know we gotta cover Tiger portion?"
Pie asked, grabbing his duffel.

"I got him. We gotta get this work," Heavy replied, pulling his bag—
and another—from the truck.

"You was ridin' round with another five hunnit stacks on you?"
Pie asked, squinting.

"I call it my emergency money," Heavy shrugged. "You never know when you might need some stupid cash, real fast."

Pie stared at him and blurted, "That's the dumbest shit I ever heard.
You gon' get yo big ass robbed."

"Well it ain't that dumb right now, is it?"
Heavy shot back.

They walked back to Ice.

"Are we all good, gentlemen?" Ice asked as his men grabbed the duffels.

"One point five mil, as agreed."

The guards opened each bag—.

nothing but thick bundles.

"I'm sure it's all there," Ice said calmly.

"To the penny," Heavy replied.

Ice nodded to the U-Haul driver. The man tossed Heavy the keys, who passed them to Pie."Oh, I gotta drive with the work, huh?" Pie joked."Until next time, gentlemen," Ice said, stepping into his ride. "Have Tiger call me when you reach him."

They watched Ice disappear into the dark."That nigga got that stupid cash!" Pie muttered, shutting up the U-Haul.

"If we paying ten per key, I can only imagine what he paying." Both shook their heads.

"The sun about to come out," Pie said. "We got this work and the streets hungry."

"Well you know what that mean, homie,".

Heavy grinned, rubbing his hands.

"It's time to make the donuts."

***

"Oh my God! **YEEES**!" Cookie moaned,
as she and Tiger made deep, hard,
passionate love on top of the covers.
"Fuck me, baby! Get it! Get it! Get it!"
she cried, pulling Tiger deeper,
meeting him thrust for thrust.

He placed her ankles on his shoulders and went deeper, sending wave after wave of trembles through her body.

26

"Yes, Daddy!" she cried out, pulling his face down to kiss him, hard.

"Turn over," he whispered.

Cookie didn't hesitate.

Face pressed into the pillow, her soft, glistening ass arched high, Tiger went in. He pulled her hips to meet every stroke. Her legs shook. Her lips quivered. Neither one could hold back—they came together, hard.

Lying in bed, Cookie was still floating. She stretched out across the satin sheets, body humming. Tiger was in the shower, rinsing off. She flipped on the TV before joining him. While digging for her nighty, she froze.

"Hey bae!" she yelled toward the bathroom "Yeah, wussup?" he called back,

while cutting off the water.

"Ain't this yo lil brotha on TV?"

Tiger stepped out in a towel, toothbrush in hand. "What you talkin bout? Who on TV?"

She pointed to the screen. He wiped his mouth, glanced up— and froze.

"Taz!" he snapped, stunned.

"Turn it up! **TURN IT UP!**"

Cookie grabbed the remote and cranked the volume as the female reporter spoke live. Kimberly Longview reported live: "This is Kimberly Longview for Channel 9 News. I'm reporting live from the scene of a

brutal homicide."

"**HOMICIDE!**" Tiger screamed.

"Sshhh!" Cookie said, turning the TV up.

A photo of the officer hit the screen as the reporter kept going. "One of Jacksonville Sheriff's Office's own, Officer Phillip

Shephard, was gunned down early this morning during what was supposed to be a routine traffic stop."

"This shit can't be real!" Tiger shouted.

"Suspect Trevor McMillan is wanted for questioning in the murder. He was the last known stop before JSO lost contact with Officer Shephard. The officer was later found dead." "This **BULLSHIT!**" Tiger snapped. "I know them crackas tape that shit! Show the **TAPE!** Cop cars got video—wzup wit that!"

"They interviewing the sheriff. See what he gotta say," Cookie said, focused on the screen. "Fuck that nigga! Fuck 'em allll!" Tiger yelled, knocking clothes off the bed as he stormed into the bathroom.

Cookie kept listening.

"Some patrol cars are still without cameras," Sheriff Hall said. "This proves why they're needed—every stop, even the smallest."

"Justice will be served. We're taking this case seriously. A reward may be offered for tips leading to an arrest or conviction."

"How many leads do you have?" Kimberly asked. "Not many. Just a license plate and a couple names."

"Trevor McMillan wouldn't be one of those names, would he?" Kimberly pressed.

"We're covering all bases. Mr. McMillan is only wanted for questioning. No solid suspects yet. But we expect updates soon."

The sheriff wrapped it up: "If you know anything about what happened here, call Crime Stoppers. A reward will be offered." Kimberly closed the segment. "Officer Shephard, 48, was a 19-year veteran of the force. He leaves behind a wife of 23 years, two sons, a daughter, and two grandchildren. He will be missed."

Cookie stood, heading to the bathroom, but Tiger came out fully dressed. She wanted to bring up the news, but her focus shifted.

"Where you think you going now, Tiger?"

Before he could answer, she snapped, "Nowhere!" and grabbed his keys, that were

sitting on the bed.

"Cookie, don't start this," he said, already pleading. "This ain't the time.

I got too much to handle."

"It's always something! You gotta handle this, you gotta handle that," she said, voice breaking. "What about me? I want attention... **I NEED... ATTENTION.**"

"Was that a threat?" Tiger asked,

picking up on her tone.

"It's a reality check...

I won't stay where I ain't wanted."

Tiger paused. Thought. "You do what you must," he said coldly, hating that she forced his hand. He grabbed his spare keys and

headed for the door.

Before leaving, he turned. "I don't wanna keep you where you don't wanna be kept."

4

Heat in the City

Pie Yay and Heavy were posted up at the spot on 22nd and Main.

"This shit startin' to give me a headache," Pie said, inhaling the coke fumes.

"Quit takin' off yo mask," Heavy snapped.

A knock hit the door.

Both of them grabbed their pistols.

"You expectin' somebody?" Heavy asked.

"If I was, I damn sure wouldn't
have 'em come here," Pie replied.

Another knock—louder, harder.

"Tiger!" they both said at once.

Outside, Tiger was anxious. He clocked the U-Haul out front with Ice's logo stamped on the side. This couldn't have come at a better time, he thought.

"**WHERE THE HELL YOU BEEN!**" Heavy barked, swinging the door open.

"Maaan," Tiger exhaled, sounding drained. "Shit's been crazy the last couple days."

Heavy led him to the back.

"Dog, we been callin' you like crazy. Even Ice been tryna reach you."

"I know, I know," Tiger said, stepping into the room where Pie was still packaging cocaine. "Finally, he decides to show up, ladies and gentlemen," Pie joked.

"Wzup, my nigga?" Tiger said, dap'n him up. "Like I told Heavy—shit's been wild.

My spot on Myrtle got hit."

"HIT?" Heavy shouted. "By the FEDS?"

"Nah, some niggas ran up in the spot,"

Tiger said.

"How the hell? Wasn't your people in there?" Pie asked.

"That's the crazy part," Tiger continued. "Whoever did it, they got let in. Then it happened. At least, that's what they say."

"Get the fuck outta here!" Heavy said with a bitter laugh. "They playin' you. I woulda wrecked shop in that bitch."

"I did," Tiger confirmed.

"What they get?" Pie asked, sealing the last bag "Three hunnit racks... and five bricks,"

Tiger muttered.

"**HEEELL NAH!**" Heavy snapped. "I woulda popped off on err'body in there."

"Who they say did it?" Pie asked.

"They say they don't know," Tiger said, stepping up to inspect the product.

"Here's what got me confused," Heavy said. "They say they don't know who did it... but they let the niggas in? That's straight bull."

"So what you did?" Pie asked, both of them expecting a grim tale.

31

Tiger paused.

Heavy cut in, sharp.

"You did handle it, didn't you?"

"Yeah, I did," Tiger mumbled.

"Okay! And—?"

Another beat passed before Tiger said,

"I shot Ace."

Heavy and Pie froze, dumbfounded.

"Your cousin Ace?" Heavy finally asked.

Tiger nodded.

"What the hell you do that for!?" Pie shouted.

"I don't know, dog!" Tiger said. "I was there... the story sounded bogus. He was in charge. I snapped. My anger took over, and I couldn't stop myself."

Silence stretched.

"Your cousin though, dog? Daaaamn," Heavy said, shaking his head.

"I know! I know! I know!" Tiger repeated, pacing. "What's really fuckin' with me is... what am I gonna tell my aunt?"

"Oh yeeeeah... Ms. Kat gonna kill you," Pie cut in "Sucks to be you right now, homie,"

Heavy added.

"Hold up!" Tiger barked. "What happened to all that, 'I woulda popped off on 'em, dog,' and 'I woulda wet err'body up that was there'?"

"All that applies to non-family members," Pie interjected, stone-faced.

"Whatever, hypocrites," Tiger muttered, reaching for a duffel bag.

"How's this separated?"

"Excuse me, sir," Pie said, stepping in. "I don't recall you puttin'

in on this, so I think this batch belongs to me and Heavy. Now, we'll gladly sell you a couple... seventeen a piece though."
He laughed.

Heavy jumped in. "First off, I only recall you payin' for a hunnit bricks. And since there's three hunnit here, two hunnit are mine. Which means I set the price."

"Thank you," Tiger said, grabbing five bags. "Just give me fifteen a piece."

They all laughed, finished packing, and dipped.

***

"I want you to pull up everything we have on a Trevor McMillan, and Robin Jeffries," Lieutenant Smith of the Jacksonville Sheriff's Office stated. Officer Mary Lovely typed in the information as requested.

"Who's Robin Jeffries?" she asked, when her picture popped up and her record was clean.

"That's what I wanna know," he said. "The last car that was reportedly stopped the night Officer Shephard was murdered was registered to her." He looked closely at the photo. "My question is, what's the relationship between these two? Is she involved somehow? Or is this just a coincidence? Either way, bring them in for questioning!"

***

Tiger was headed to Ken Knight to holla at DJ, to drop off some work, when Cookie called. She said it was important and needed him home. His first instinct was to ignore her request, but something told him to swing by—even if just to stash a few of those keys.

When he walked through the door, Cookie met him with eyes full of tears. She ran up, threw her arms around him, and held tight. "Baby, I am sooo sorry," she pleaded between sniffs. "I didn't know. Please forgive me."

Tiger stood still, hesitant and stunned.

What did she know that she was sorry for not knowing earlier?

"It's okay, bae," he said, cautiously.

"How you handling it?"

What the hell did she know? he thought, completely stumped.

"I'm good. I guess,"

he said, as he was heading to their room.

"I'm sorry again," she pleaded, pressing her chest. "I just saw it on the news."

Okay... now I'm lost for real, Tiger thought. "What was on the news?" he finally asked, unable to take the suspense.

"Your cousin, Ace!"

Tiger's eyes widened. What could she have seen or heard about Ace?

"He's dead!" she said, pausing for a reaction. "They found his body in a ditch,

by 45th and Moncrief."

That threw Tiger. He knew they'd handled the body. But the ditch—and 45th?

He paused for a second. That was brilliant. No way it could link back to him with the body found that far away.

Plus, it would make the 45th area hot. All the smokers would shift toward 16th.

That was good for business.

But there was one thing Tiger dreaded most about all this—his aunt.

How the hell am I gonna tell her?, He thought. Before he left, he hid forty keys deep in the garage and took sixty with him to drop off.

***

Tiger was getting much love riding through Ken Knight. The streets knew when Tiger pulled up, money followed. All the small-time dope boys waited for his drop—because they knew he always made one stop in the hood: DJ's spot. "There go my nigga!"

DJ yelled as Tiger pulled up.

DJ was in the front yard, talking to Keisha, who was doing Lisa's hair for the club that night. DJ waved for Tiger to come inside.

Tiger hated people in his business, and too many were out today. Even uninvited eyes were lurking. Parked across from DJ's house, in a smoke-grey Ford Focus, sat Detective Mark Anthony Holzendorf—a highly decorated federal agent who'd been watching DJ for some time. He could've brought him in on sales, possession, or felon-with-firearm charges. But he wasn't after DJ. He wanted DJ's connect.

A few years back, DJ had come home from an eight-year bid and jumped straight back on top. Holzendorf knew the only way to stop it was to take out the head. Cut the head, the body dies. DJ walked into the apartment and came out with a red Transformers bookbag. Holzendorf had been staking the field for hours, snapping photos. Nothing major yet. He almost called it, but decided to wait it out.

Tiger watched as Keisha stopped DJ on his way to the truck. He was sure the convo was about him by the way Keisha kept glancing over and smiling. DJ must've given her the green light, because right after he spoke,

her grin got even brighter.

"Here he come trying to throw this ghetto hood rat on me," Tiger mumbled to himself.

"Wzup, big homie?"

DJ stated, climbing into Tiger's truck.

"I can't call it," Tiger responded, giving him dap. He reached into the back and pulled up two duffel bags—one for DJ, the other for Big Lez. "That's me right there?" DJ asked as Tiger handed him the duffel.

"**OOOWEE!**" DJ said, excited, cracking it open and catching the smell of the cocaine.

"That's That Thang!" he added.

"Now, let me get that cash out ya," Tiger said.

DJ handed over the other bag and kept inspecting the goods.

"Transformers, huh?" Tiger asked, clocking the bag DJ brought.

"That's my son bag," DJ replied.

"He left it here the other day. Kinda hope I can get that back A.S.A.P."

Tiger popped the bag open, scanned the bundles. "Is this three-fifty?"

"Nah!" DJ huffed. "That's one-seventy five." He checked the coke again.

"Damn dog! Yo prices sky rocketed like a mug... Wzup wit dat? They were seventeen-five! Now how much are they?"

"They still seventeen-five," Tiger cut in. "Last time we talked, you said shit was bammin so hard you wanted to upgrade to twenty bricks."

Tiger reached for the duffel DJ had.

"What you doing?" DJ snapped.

"Taking ten bricks out, and leaving you wit the ten you paid for... I hope you don't think I'mma front the other ten?" Tiger laughed.

"Nah, I got the cash," DJ said.

"This right on time," DJ added, shaking the bag. "Wait right here."

DJ hopped out the truck and headed inside to grab Tiger's money. Keisha stopped him again. Detective Holzendorf, parked nearby, watched Dj exit the house with one bag and reenter with another. "Now we seem to be getting somewhere", he mumbled, snapping pics of Tiger's tinted truck.

Ten minutes later, Dj returned. Tiger leaned back, observing Keisha and Lisa—catching glances and giggles at Tiger. He smirked at their boldness. *I should snatch up both of 'em and let the team run through 'em*, he thought, smiling as Dj reappeared and Keisha blocked the path again.

Detective Holzendorf noticed DJ carrying a pink backpack along with another empty duffel. "This one-fifty," DJ explained as he entered the truck. "I got the rest, just not here."
Tiger nodded in understanding. "Just holla at me later on," he said, opening the bag.
"I brought yo big ass bag back, so you can give me back my shorties' bags," DJ added.
Tiger dumped the money into his duffel and handed DJ his bags.
"Hannah Montana, huh?" Tiger asked, eyeing the pink bag.
"You know that's my daughter bag," DJ defended with a smile.
"If you say so,"
Tiger replied with a smile of his own.

Tiger was about to go when DJ remembered Keisha's request. "I almost forgot, big homie! Lil Red
wanna holla at ya."
He could see the hesitation in Tiger's face. He'd already told Keisha he'd make it happen, so now he had to seal the deal.
"I heard she had that stupid head!" DJ added, trying to bait him.

Tiger took an extra minute to think. He knew plenty girls with FYIAH head. *She also like girls.* Ding ding ding, we have a winner.

37

A light went off in Tiger's head and he agreed.

"Just give her my other cell phone number," Tiger said.

"Nah, get out and come holla at her. She heard of ya, seen you around, now she wanna meet ya. Tiger let out a heavy sigh.

"Maaan! Come on and get this new ass... At least come say hey. A lil conversation ain't gonna hurt," DJ pushed. "Come say a few words, then later on give her and her home girl that meat, and then keep it movin."

Tiger watched how Keisha moved around. *Ghetto*, he thought. *All she want is to feel like she's that chic for a minute, that's all.*

DJ opened his door, about to get out, then looked back. "You coming?"

"Yeah. Here I come," Tiger confirmed.

Tiger reached in his armrest and threw on his cubed-shared diamond and platinum bracelet, along with the matching chain and six-inch diamond-encrusted cross. He watched as DJ stood beside Keisha, leaned in, and said something that made both her and Lisa blush.

Moments later, Tiger stepped out.

He was everything a girl like Keisha dreamed about. DOPEBOY—clean kicks, heavy jewelry, and a name that rang through the streets. She figured all it'd take was a few photo ops and some bomb sex to raise her stock. She knew the deal: this was a fast track to her fifteen minutes. And she knew one thing about the game—smaller dope boys always wanted what the big dogs had, and they'd pay to get it.

Tiger was also everything Detective Holzendorf had been hunting for.

A promotion.

***

Click. Click. Click. Holzendorf took photos from every angle.

Tiger with Keisha. Tiger with her friend. But the money shot? Tiger and DJ grinning, DJ holding the same book bags he'd stepped out with earlier. "So I guess you that dude, huh?" The detective muttered with a smirk.

"Well say cheese. You on candid camera.."

***

   "So you Tiger, huh?" KKeishabegan.

"Yeah, I'm Tiger," he spoke, looking around at his surroundings. Without realizing, he glanced straight at Detective Holzendorf's car tucked in the cut—but brushed it off.

"So what you getting into later on?" Lisa cut in. "I guess I'm getting into yall," he added, with the oldest line in the book.

"I Know That's Right!" they both spoke.

"Shiiit. It's whatever," Keisha said, already feelin' the vibe.

   "We were suppose to be hitting the club tonight and getting our drank on," Lisa added.

"You and a couple of yo homeboys can meet us! We'll have one more girl wit us."

"WHO!" Keisha asked, patting her head so she wouldn't scratch her hairdo.

"Sasha."

Keisha thought for a moment. "Oh yeah! She bout that."

"What club yall going to?" Tiger asked. "PLUSH," they both said, grinding the air.

"Nah! We don't do Plush. That's for jits."

"Well it's whatever," Keisha replied. "I just wanna get out and have fun."

   "Cool! Peep this," Tiger said. "My homeboy owns Club Heavy, and this weekend Rick Ross gonna be there."

"You Gone Get Us In Free?" Lisa asked, already knowing she
ain't have money for that.
"Hit me up later this week and yall
can be my guests."
They both nodded quick.
"So I gotta wait til this weekend to see you again?" KKeishaasked.

"Unfortunately yeah... Gotta busy week."
    Tiger reached in his pocket, pulled out his keys, and hit the
automatic start. The truck started up like magic. Keisha and
Lisa lit up like he was David Blaine.
Lord they ghetto, he thought as he headed toward the driver's
side.
"Damn he fine," Keisha mumbled, thinking she said it low—but
he heard her.
"Bye Boo!" she called, still watching like a hawk as he pulled
off. Tiger drove off, same direction Detective Holzendorf was
parked.
Holzendorf tracked him with the camera, snapping shots of
Tiger's plates.
"Don't get too comfortable, whoever you are," the detective
muttered,
watching him disappear down the block. "Cause one false
move—and yo ass is mine."

5

Queen Pin

Tiger left Ken Knight Ave., heading to Washington Heights Apartments, where Big Lez was. Big Lez was the Queen Pin of Tiger's organization. All-around dime piece—she could have any man she wanted, and any girl too. She loved her some Tiger, and she'd do anything to prove her loyalty. And on several occasions, she had proven how loyal she was.

About six months back, Tiger hit her line around three in the morning while she was laid up with her, at-the-time, boy toy. They had just finished a heated sex session. Normally, no matter what time it was, she never stayed the night at nobody's house but her own. But she was feelin' Mike heavy. She considered him her main—her boo boo.

Not to get it twisted with her boo, Tiger.

"Wzup, boo," Big Lez said, sitting up in the bed after hearing Tiger's voice.

"Nah, you good, baby." She stood up, walking her naked body across the room to grab

her slip off the TV.

"I wasn't doing nuttin anyway,

just laying down."

Mike heard her talking and got hot.

"Who the hell is that?" he snapped.

Lez turned her back to him,

trying to hear Tiger better.

"Sure baby, I can do that. You know I got you," she said with a smile.

"WHO THE FUCK IS THAT!"

Mike kept pushing, voice rising.

"SHUT...UP!" Lez yelled, holding the phone to her chest. "Don't you see me on the phone?"Mike was ready to lose it. Ain't nobody disrespected him like that before—especially not in his own crib.

"I'm back, boo," Lez continued.

"That ain't nobody. Now, what you said?"

Tiger had a situation, and he needed Big Lez to handle it.

"I sure can, baby. Gimme 'bout an hour or so—I gotta run to the house."

"You ain't going nowhere!" Mike snapped, stepping out the bed.

"Hold on, boo," Lez told Tiger.

She could hear him yelling through the phone, threatening to come over and shut Mike up himself—permanently.

She wasn't letting it get to that point. She was gon' handle it right now.

"You might wanna sit yo ass down somewhere," she said, turning to Mike. "I like ya, but you on some other shit right now, talkin' bout this one like that."

She held the phone out so he could see—whoever was on the line was way more important than him.

"WHAT BITCH?!" Mike blurted.

"Fuck that nigga!"

Tiger heard it. Lez could hear him snap, screaming threats through the line. She could almost stomach being called a bitch—she already called herself the queen bitch. But *"fuck that nigga"*? Nah. That shit wasn't finna slide. She quietly walked over to her clothes. Inside her jacket pocket was her .38.

"Oh, so now you fenta go cause I said,

Fuck that—"

Pow. Pow.

Before he could finish, Lez put two in his chest. Mike dropped back,

sprawled out in his bed—naked.

"I'm back, boo," Lez continued with Tiger.

"Like I said, gimme an hour, or so."

She hung up and looked around for her clothes.

One of her Jimmy Choo heels had

blood specks on it.

"Oh hell nah. This ain't gon' work,"

she said sarcastically.

"These six-hundred-dollar shoes."

She spotted the shoebox he'd bragged about before. Inside was a platinum diamond chain with a cross charm, a matching bracelet, and ten stacks in cash.

"Okay, baby. Momma forgive ya," she said, getting dressed. She was about to walk out when she turned back and said, with a smirk,

"I know you mad at me, so I'mma let you lay there and cool off... I hope you call me later. But if you don't, I understand."

She blew his body a kiss, and left.

Later that day, when she saw Tiger, she gave him the necklace.

***

Tiger pulled up in front of Lez's apartment. He spotted her pearl-white Bentley sport with white backdrop floaters. Parked next to it was a red F-150 and a blue bubble Chevy tagged with a yellow Napa Auto Parts logo. Inside the Chevy, two dudes were deep in a smoke session, bumpin' Plies. Tiger was sure he recognized one of them, but couldn't quite place it. He figured Lez had company. He didn't wanna interrupt her while she was getting money—but he damn sure wasn't about to haul a duffel bag full of coke upstairs. He hit her line and let her know he was outside.

"Aahite fellas, time to pack it up," Big Lez told Chad and Taz.

She had on black tights—no panties—a white and black Bebe tank, and some black, white, and pink #5 Jordans.

"Wzup wit me and you?" Taz said, grabbing at her as she tried to push them toward the door. "The only thing that's up between me and you is your dick," she shot back, noticing he was getting aroused. "So put it down and get out." "You put it down," he kept on, getting bolder. "You betta stop before I cut it off."

Taz grinned devilish.

"Stop, Taz! You play too much," she snapped, shoving him against the door.

"Now, I said I'mma call you when I'm done cookin' up yo shit."

Taz had dropped off four ounces of coke for her to whip into crack.

"I'mma holla at ya in a few," he said with a smirk. "You gonna gimme that pussy!"

"You don't make enough yet," she clapped back, letting him out the back door.

Lez ran into the room and changed into white boy shorts but kept the tank top on. She kicked off her Jordans, left the socks. She always made sure to look sexy for Tiger. Seconds

44

later, he knocked and stepped inside. He'd just missed Taz by a few seconds. Lez came out the back half-naked and smelling good. Tiger tried to walk past, but she blocked the walkway just enough that he had to brush against her. He dropped the bag on the floor in front of the couch and sat down. Lez stood in front of him with her back turned.

"So what's in the bag?" she asked sarcastically, bending over slow.

"I know what you tryin' to do, Lez," Tiger said, smirking. "Got too much to do right now. Gotta get in and get out."

"Oooh yeah... that's what I want you to do," she purred, switching into her sexy voice.

"Get in, and get out... and in, and out, and in, and ooooh..." She moaned like she was mid-orgasm. "As much as I'd love to give you this meat,

I gotta go," he said, standing up.

She pushed him back onto the couch and straddled him.

"Not even for a little while, Daddy?" she teased.

"Ahite now. Keep that daddy shit up, you gon' write a check ya ass can't cash."

He stood again, lifting her with him.

"Oh, I cash checks," she said, pulling him toward the back room.

"I can't stay, Lez," Tiger half-whined, even though he wanted to.

"I'm not talkin' 'bout that." She popped open a Gucci luggage case, flashing stacks of money. "That's three hunnit stacks in there?" he asked. "Actually, it's five hunnit," she replied.

"Why you got that much money round here? Matter fact, why even on you?"

"I'm good, Daddy," she cooed, flipping to her baby voice.

She pulled her trusty .38 from under the pillow and laid it at the foot of the bed.

"I ain't got time to count all that," Tiger said. "I'll just swing through later. Just have it ready."

He turned to leave, but she chased him.

"I want some sex. NOW. It's been two months." "Whaaaat!" Tiger joked. "That gotta be a record for you?"

"It is!" she snapped back.

"You and I—on the beach—that was the last time I had some." Tiger nodded but kept toward the door. She rushed over again.

"You seriously gon' leave me like this?"

Tiger paused as Lez hit him with a rapid-fire set of sad faces.

"Yep!" he said, pecked her on the forehead, and walked out.

"PUUUUNK!" she screamed through the door, laughing.

Since Tiger was gone, she figured it was the perfect time to finish cooking Taz's cocaine. She gathered everything she needed, but just as she got started, there was a knock at the door. She wasn't expecting nobody else—had to be Tiger. Smiling, she adjusted her breasts on the way to the door.

"I knew you'd be back!" she grinned, swinging it open.

Her face dropped. "Oh, it's you, Taz."

She turned and walked back to the stove.

"Why you back so early? I told you I'd call when I was done."

Taz followed, eyes locked on her ass.

"I know! I ain't come here for that," he said, still staring.

"Then what you want, Taz?" She spun around and caught his eyes glued to her curves. She looked down, realizing she was still

46

dressed for Tiger.

"You gotta go!" she snapped. "I said I'd call you." "Fuck that, yo!" he barked. "I came here for us." "There is no us, Taz! Never was, never will be." She tried pushing him toward the door again, like before—but this time he didn't budge. "Aahite, lil boy. You startin' to piss me off!" she warned, trying to yank away. She kept her cool—he was Tiger's little brother.

"I told you earlier, you gon' gimme that—"

Before he could finish, Big Lez drove her knee into his crotch. It didn't drop him, but gave her just enough time to break loose and run for her room. Taz was right behind her. Lez lunged for the .38 on the bed, but just as she turned to aim, he was already on her—smacking it from her hand with his left. He followed with a right hook to her face, sending her flying back onto the bed. She bounced right up—swinging and scratching like hell.

"**BITCH!**" he yelled, breaking free from her scratches and punches. Realizing he was bigger, he charged in with a fierce punch, knocking her into a daze. He glanced over at the floor and saw her .38.

"Cute," he smiled.

He turned back toward Lez, then felt his face. Blood was on his hand. "Crazy bitch," he huffed.

Seeing her dazed gave him an evil idea. He started rubbing up her leg, trying to pull her shorts off. When Taz got close enough, Lez kneed him in the stomach and tried to gouge at his eyes.

"Muthafucka!" he yelled, breaking from her grip. Without hesitation, he grabbed her gun and—**POW**—shot her in the stomach.

For a brief moment, he felt like he went too far. Then again, *I was defending myself*, he thought. Looking around her room in a slight panic, he noticed the Gucci luggage half open. When he pulled it the rest of the way, his eyes widened at the wads of cash.

"**HEEEELL YEAH!**" he screamed, grinning.

An agonizing moan came out of Big Lez, alerting him she was still alive. Barely.

"Thanks for the cash, ma," he said, about to dip. But something made him double back. He looked over at Lez, bleeding, helpless. Walked over to her body.

He rubbed up her leg again. This time, there wasn't much of a fight. He lifted her legs onto his shoulders, pulled off her shorts, and forcefully inserted himself.

"I told you I would get that pussy," he said, as he continued to rape Lez.

When he was done, he looked down at her barely breathing— and shot her again to finish the job.

***

"Who is it?" Robin stated, hearing someone at the door.

"It's the police! Could you open up, ma'am?" one of the Jacksonville Sheriff's officers replied. Robin placed the chain on the door and opened it as far as the chain would allow.

"Yes, may I help you?" she asked through the narrow space.

"Robin Jeffries?" the lady cop asked.

"Yes."

"Could you open up, ma'am, so we could talk with you?" the male cop followed.

"My husband's not home, and I'm here alone with my daughter," she said. "What is this about? And who are you?"

"I'm officer Daniels,
and this is officer Elaine Smith.
We just need to ask you a couple questions."

"About?" Robin shot back.

"Ma'am... the door," officer Daniels urged.

"It's just a few questions."

After a few seconds, she removed the chain and opened the door fully.

"Now, what is this about?"

she asked, arms crossed.

"Ma'am, do you know a Trevor McMillan?" Daniels asked.

"Trevor who?" Robin blinked, confused.

"Trevor McMillan."

"Who is he?" Robin responded instantly.

"Ma'am, we were hoping you could tell us," officer Smith cut in.

"Never heard of him," Robin said flatly.

"What? He know me?"

Neither officer answered.

They politely moved on.

"Are you the owner of a 2001 Dodge Stratus?" "Yes, I am!" Robin replied, confused.

"Where's my car? What happened to my car?"

"Have you loaned your car to anyone in the past few days?" Officer Elaine asked.

"My brother—why?"

Before they could ask another question, Robin jumped in. "Bump all that! Where's my car?

And where's my brother?"

"Ma'am, we believe if we find your brother, we'll find your car," Officer Daniels replied.

"What do you mean, find my brother? What has he done?"

After a moment of hesitation,

Officer Elaine stated, "We have reason to believe your brother may have been involved in the murder of a J.S.O. officer."

Robin's eyes widened. Her mouth dropped.

"Oh my God."

"Have you talked with your brother recently?" Daniels asked.

"Not since yesterday, when he came and
got my car."

"What is your brother's name?"

Officer Elaine asked.

"Larry Long... we call him Spanky,"
Robin admitted.

After writing the information down, Officer Elaine asked, "You wouldn't happen to have a picture of your brother, would ya?"

"No! I don't," Robin stated, shaking her head.

They were about to wrap up when Officer Daniels handed Robin his business card.

"If you see or talk with him, please contact me," he said, pointing to his personal number.

"I understand this your brother and you wanna protect him," he continued,

"but he may not be involved. So the earlier he contacts us, the better it'll be for him."

Robin nodded.

"So, do you feel Trevor McMillan is a friend of your brother?" Officer Elaine asked.

"Could be," Robin replied nonchalantly.

"Well, we thank you for your time," Officer Daniels said as they walked off.

Robin stared down at the card.

"I'm not callin you 'bout my brotha," she muttered, ripping it in half.

"But when I see Spank..." She balled her fist in anger. "I'mm kick his ass."

6

Blood Ain't Always Thicker

Tiger had just gotten off the phone with Heavy. He was trying to meet up to give him his money. Heavy said he was in Daytona and would be back in the morning. Tiger agreed to bring it to the club tomorrow night. He was looking forward to the Rick Ross concert at Club Heavy's—but not to talking with his aunt. The longer he waited, the worse it would get.

He pulled into his aunt's yard just as Cookie was calling him. "Wzup, baby?" he answered, heavy-hearted. "I'm at my aunt Kat house."

Cookie was wondering when he'd be home but changed up once she found out where he was. She told him if she wasn't there when he got back, she might still be at the mall, hunting for an outfit for the concert tomorrow.

As he got out the truck, his aunt came out of the house.

"I was wondering who that was with all that boopy-de-boop noise."

"My bad, auntie," Tiger said with a smile.

He walked over and gave her a hug and kiss on the cheek.

"What you was up to?" he asked.

"Nuttin! Just tired... Bout ready to go to work," she replied, sitting down on the porch.

"What time you gotta be there?"

"I actually called in, told 'em I'mma be late. **"WHY?"** Tiger asked, as Ms. Kat ran back inside. Moments later, she returned holding a little girl, about three years old.

"Who do we have here, auntie?"

Tiger asked, smiling.

"This Ace lil girl," she said, trying to turn her toward him. "You never met her."

"Nah, I haven't," Tiger replied, the guilt setting in. She looked just like Ace.

"I'm not too fond of his baby momma," Ms. Kat added, rocking the child gently.

"What's her name?"

"Tamela... Tamela Porter," she said with a smile. "She's beautiful," Tiger whispered, eyes almost tearing up.

Baby Tamela heard a male voice and turned to see who it was.

"Da..dee... want my dadee."

"I want your da..dee too," Aunt Kat replied, mimicking little Tamela.

"As I was saying, her momma is one of them lil party girls. The only time she want something to do with her is when child services do their re-evaluation."

"So you keep her?" Tiger asked.

"May as well say I do. I have her all day and night, unless I'm at work," she said. "Ace know what time I have to be at work. He usually be here! Cause I can't call in again."

Tiger knew Ace wasn't coming, but he didn't know how to tell her. Not yet anyway.

"He prolly wit that damn girl... Oooo Lord, forgive me," she snapped. "See what I mean? She got me losing my religion."

"Cup, cup," little Tamela woke up,

wanting her cup.

"Gimme a minute, baby," Ms. Kat said, walking into the house.

While she was inside, Margie, the neighborhoods most popular crack head, came strolling toward them. Several years ago, she used to be one of the sexiest women in the neighborhood. A sight for sore eyes. Now-a-days she's a sight to make your eyes sore. Ms. Kat came out just in time to see Margie walk in her yard.

"Oh my lord! What do she want?" Ms. Kat mumbled to Tiger. "What do you want, Monica? I don't have any money or cigarettes!"

"No Ms. Kat, I'm here for you sweetie,

How are you?"

"I'm fine, Monica... Just waitin on Ace to come get this baby, so I can get to work."

Monica placed her hand over her mouth, attempting to hold back tears. Tiger confirmed she knew something, but what? And where did she get her info from?

"So you haven't heard?" she stated, with a discouraged look on her face.

"Heard what, Margie?"

"**MARGIE**!" Tiger yelled, waking Tamela up. "look What You Done, Tiger!" Ms. Kat snapped, as Tamela began to whine. She got up and walked in the house to calm Tamela down.

Tiger turned his attention to Margie and, with a stern voice, asked,

"So what do you know!"

"Well, I know that blood's not thicker than water to some people," she said sarcastically.

54

"What you trying to say?" Tiger played dumb "Come on, T! You should know by now—I am the streets.
I know all that happens, and who did it."

"All like what?" Tiger cut in.

"Let's cut the bull. You know that I know what I know," she stated. "But I take it Ms. Kat don't know... and you wanna keep it that way, huh?" "We gonna keep it that way!" Tiger demanded.

"I totally agree. There's no reason info like this should ever get out." She slowly held out her hand. "The Lord said He will provide,"

Margie began jokingly. "I was so worried on how I was gonna get my lights paid. But the Lord said He'll make a way."

Tiger knew he was being extorted. And he knew damn well she wasn't putting that money on no lights. Still, he reached in his pocket and peeled off two hundred-dollar bills. When he tried to hand them over, she kept her hand out and cleared her throat—like, 'come a lil better.' He dropped in two more fifties.

She glanced at the money, then back at him, and started singing, "We're almost theeere looord. We're aaalmost theeeere..."

"You better close your damn fist before I close it for ya!" Tiger snapped.

She snatched the money with an attitude. "Let me take my money before I end up in a ditch somewhere."

She was about to walk off, then turned and asked, "You ain't got no crack on ya, do ya?"Tiger mean-mugged her and walked back to his aunt's porch.

Ms. Kat came back outside without Tamela."Where's lil momma?" Tiger asked.

"I put her in the bed. She heavy."

"Auntie," Tiger began, nervous. "If you want, I'll take my lil cuzin wit me, and give you a break." "No, baby. This Ace's responsibility, and he gonna watch her. Ima just call in and wait for Ace to call or come home."

Tiger felt like crap. He reached in his pocket again and pulled out a knot of cash. He knew it had to be at least five grand. He tried handing it to his aunt.

"Now chile, you know I can't take that money... It's not of the Lord," she preached.

"Well, don't the Bible say suttin' 'bout bad money getting to the righteous, or suttin' like that?" he shot back.

"Don't come here trying to use my Bible against me," she laughed.

Tiger watched her—happy but tired. The last thing she needed was to know her son was dead. Not yet.

"Well, I gotta go, Auntie," he said, knowing now wasn't the time. "I know you got a soda or something I can get?"

"Sure do. Come on in," she said, standing up "Nah, I'm good," he replied, hitting the truck's automatic start. "Gotta watch the truck."

She walked inside. The moment she was out of view, Tiger dropped the money on the chair, ran to his truck, and dipped.

When she came back out, she saw the stack sitting there and caught Tiger on the corner, pulling off. He blew his horn and waved as he crossed the intersection and disappeared from view.

Ms. Kat smiled, shook her head, looked down at the money, and said,

"Bless his heart, Lord... bless his heart."

***

Tiger had attempted several times to contact Big Lez, but got no answer. Odd, he thought. She never ignored his calls. He was starting to worry. They were supposed to meet so he could pick up his money, but her phone kept going straight to voicemail. Tiger had been running and ripping for the last few days, and he needed some rest. He decided to head home and lay low for a while.

When he pulled into his yard, he noticed Cookie hadn't made it back yet. Perfect. No better time to get some real rest—without her nagging about something petty.

***

Detective Holzendorf got back to the Federal agency hyped. Finally—something he could use to put a permanent end to DJ and the Ken Knight/North Side drug war for good. He downloaded the pictures he'd taken earlier and had a screening run to ID the other guy in the photo with DJ.

"Antonio McMillan," the detective muttered, tapping his desk. "No recent records... no drug charges... just a couple petty theft and vandalism raps as a minor."

He nodded slowly, eyes locked on Tiger's picture. "I see what I gotta do to get you."

Leaning back in his chair, he twirled a pencil between his fingers, still studying the image. "Mr. Antonio McMillan... you not as clean as you pretend to be."

He zoomed in on the shot of DJ holding the duffel bags. Holzendorf was sure—either money or dope was in those bags. And if that was true, Tiger was DJ's plug. His promotion.

"You and I are gonna get real close," he smirked, scrolling through the pictures. "Reeeeeal close.

***

Tiger woke hours later to his phone buzzing. "Hello?" he

slurred, voice thick with sleep.

It was Cookie. She'd finished her shopping and wanted to know when he'd be home.

"I'm here now," he said.

"Be naked!" was her final word,

then she hung up.

He glanced at his watch—four hours had slipped by and still no word from Lez.

In the bathroom, his phone rang again. He stared at the screen. 'What, Cookie?' he muttered, heading toward it.

"Who dis?" he answered, surprised by the unknown number. He didn't give that number to many—had to be family.

"It's Shands Hospital. We have a Leslie Hill on your emergency list."

"Big Lez!" Tiger panicked. "Is she okay? What happened?"

"I hate to inform you... she's been shot several times in the abdomen and—"

Before the receptionist could finish, Tiger screamed, **"FUUUU-UCK!"** He clutched the phone, pain cracking his chest.

"Is she gonna be okay?"

"She's been in surgery for a few hours now," came the calm response.

"I'm on my way," he cut in, voice urgent. He hung up before she could say more.

Tiger stormed out in a panic just as Cookie pulled up.

"I thought you were laying down," she started. "Where you think you going now, Tiger?"

"Baby, I gotta run to the hospital," he replied, pushing past her. "Big Lez was shot!"

"OH GOD, no!" Cookie clasped her chest, panic ripping through

58

her.

"Is she okay? What hospital she at?" Cookie bombarded him, but Tiger said nothing.**"DAMNIT!! I'LL CALL YOU WHEN I FIND OUT SOMETHING, OKAY!"**

His tone was sharp—cold even. Cookie recoiled, stunned by how hard he'd snapped—over another woman. Even if it was Big Lez.

Cookie backed away, shaky and teary. Tiger called after her: "Baby!"

But she pushed inside. "Cookie!" he yelled. "I'M-sorry," he whispered,

hoping she'd come back.

He glanced at the driveway. Every second counted. Big Lez needed him now.

***

Pulling up at the hospital, Tiger couldn't shake the feeling that Lez getting shot was his fault. He let her do too much, deal with too many sheisty dudes—without the protection she deserved. As much as she'd held him down, he felt he failed her. Inside, his heart pounded like a drumline. He rushed into the Emergency Room and found the receptionist.

"What floor is Leslie Hill on?"

he asked, breath short.

"She's on the fourth floor. Intensive care," the receptionist answered.

He hit the elevator hard, bolting up to the fourth. At the desk, he didn't waste time.

"Leslie Hill's room, please."

The nurse checked her chart, glanced back up. "Ms. Hill is in the Intensive Care Recovery Unit."

"I understand that, ma'am.

I just need the room number."

"She can't have any visitors at this time—""**THAT'S BULL!**"

Tiger exploded before reeling it back. He took a breath.

"Ma'am... she needs me," he said,

voice low but urgent.

The nurse softened, but held the line.

"Sir, she was the victim of a shooting. We can't allow visitors until police clear the investigation."

Tiger started pacing, fists clenched.

"Is there a doctor—anybody I can talk to? I just need to know how she doin'."

She double-checked the chart. "Dr. Robinson is her attending. I'll page him for you.

Please have a seat."

Tiger dropped into a chair, overwhelmed. "What if she dies? I couldn't live with myself," he muttered, tapping the back of his head

with his fists.

Then—"This looks all too familiar," a voice said above him.

Tiger looked up. Stunned.

"Taz?" he said slowly, his face tightening.

"That don't sound like a happy-to-see-me look," Taz smirked.

"It's just been a while, that's all," Tiger said.

"A loooong while."

Four years ago, Tiger and Taz had a major falling out—and they hadn't spoken since. Back then, Tiger was fresh in the hustle, before Ice. He dealt through an Italian connect named Juarez. Juarez was big-time—and he didn't mix with colored folks. His cousin Jose' sold ounces to Tiger.

They got caught in a rental car on the south side—with nine ounces of coke in the trunk. Jose' was driving, the police knew it

60

was his—but Tiger stayed quiet. Jose' denied knowing too. Weeks later, Jose' got popped again—this time with three guns, a thousand ecstasy pills, and a half-kilo. He got eight years. Tiger lost his connect. But Juarez saw Tiger moving around, remembered him from rolling with Jose'—recognized he was stand-up.

Tiger wanted badly to put Taz on with him, so he and his brother could take over. He finally introduced Taz to Juarez. One day, Tiger sent Taz to pick up two kilos from Juarez. When Juarez showed up, Taz robbed him—and threatened to kill him if he ever came back to Jacksonville.

Tiger called Juarez after not seeing Taz for days. Juarez told him he had a $10,000 bounty on Taz's head unless Tiger paid for the two kilos—plus another $10,000 for the disrespect. He ended the call screaming "monkey this" and "coon that."
Tiger finally got ahold of Taz and asked about the accusations. Taz didn't even try to deny it. All Tiger wanted was the $45,000 he'd given Taz for Juarez. He'd figure something out about the extra ten.

Tiger agreed to meet Juarez at Metropolitan Park to pay the money. Taz, thinking it was a bad idea, followed Tiger and hid nearby. He overheard the conversation and didn't like what Juarez was saying. Juarez kept ranting about how he don't fuck with monkeys. Tiger was getting heated—especially since he was trying to make it right.

Sensing Tiger's anger, Juarez pulled out his gun and laid it across his lap, pointed at Tiger. Taz crept up from behind one of the bridge posts and put two bullets in the back of Juarez's head.

Taz started calling Tiger soft and all kinds of other names. Tiger told him, when you play the game foul, foul shit happens in return. Taz wasn't trying to hear that. He said he and Tiger had nothing in common, and they may as
well part ways.

61

Taz took his two kilos, moved to the South Side—and blew almost all of it. He met Spanky and Champ, and made robbing his hustle. Tiger met Heavy and Pie-Yay. Soon after, he met Ice—and blew up.

"How ya been?" Taz asked.

"I'm good."

"Well, ya look good," Taz continued.

"What do you want, Taz?" Tiger snapped.

"Is that how you treat your lil brotha?" Taz asked, sarcastically.

Tiger looked at Taz with a crazy look on his face. "What are you doing out here anyway?"

he wondered.

Taz pulled back, thought for a moment.

"I'm here for the same reason you are... To see Big Lez. I knew her too."

"Yeah, she was shot," Tiger cut in.

"I know! I mean, I heard," Taz responded.

Tiger caught the slip—but paid it no mind.

"Who told you?" Tiger wondered.

"Come on, man," Taz tried to redirect.

"I'm still in touch with the streets."

"I bet you are," Tiger added.

"I saw you on Channel 9 news. I guess you trying to be a movie star, huh?"

"What's that supposed to mean?"

"I saw you on the news, that's what it mean... You wanted for shooting a cop."

"You really think I did that shit?" Taz whined.

"I don't know what to think right now, bruh. My main concern is Lez."

"There ya go again wit that shit," Taz cut in. "What shit, Taz?

62

Huh? What shit?" Tiger jumped in his face.

"**THIS!** Overreacting, caring too much shit," Taz pointed out.

"Go to hell!" Tiger snapped.

"Go to hell, huh?" Taz laughed.

"Cool... You still soft, I see."

Tiger charged at Taz, jacked him up, and pinned him to the wall.

"There's that anger," Taz said, jokingly "Unfortunately, bruh... I'm not the enemy."

Tiger paused. After realizing what he was doing, he let Taz go. As he sat back down, he muttered: "She's so young... This all my fault."

"Bruh, one thing I found out being in these streets," Taz began. "It's like a chess game. And when you the king, you gotta be willing to sacrifice any piece."

He paused as Tiger lifted his head.

"Even the queen."

"Nah," Tiger snapped, shaking his head.

"Not her."

Doctor Robinson came out and walked over to Taz and Tiger.

"Are you all here for Leslie Hill?"

They both nodded yes.

"How is she, Doc?" Tiger asked, concerned.

"Ms. Hill came in with two bullet wounds to the abdomen. We operated and removed both bullets, and she should be fine."

Tiger was about to let out a sigh of relief, when the doctor added—

"But... not the babies."

"**BABIES!**" Tiger blurted. "Did you say babies?" "Yes, Mr. Hill. Your wife was eight weeks pregnant—with twins."

Both Tiger and Taz looked stunned.

63

"Each baby was hit with a bullet. That alone is what saved your wife from any extensive internal damage."

Tiger struggled to hold back tears.

"C-c-can I see her?"

"She needs her rest," the doctor started. "She's in recovery right now."

Tiger finally exhaled, a partial relief. But the doctor wasn't done.

"There's one more thing we discovered during surgery," he continued.

"Mrs. Hill's pelvic wall tissue was torn pretty badly."

"What that mean, doc?" Tiger asked, alarmed. "Well, basically... what I'm trying to say is..."

The doctor paused, steadying his voice.

"Outside of being shot... your wife was raped also."

Tiger eased away from the doctor, disgust rising in his throat. He turned and walked toward the elevator, with Taz close behind.

Taz knew, eventually Lez would be up and talking—and he wanted her dead. A.S.A.P.

"Ima kill every nigga involved," Tiger snapped, swinging in the air as he and Taz waited for the elevator.

He glanced over at Taz, eyes bloodshot red. Taz could clearly see the fire burning in Tiger's stare. He knew—if word of his involvement ever came out, it was over. He had to hurry up and kill Lez... or worse. He might have to kill Tiger.

7

Devil in Disguise

Tiger was woken up the next morning by breaking news on Channel 9. Kimberly Longview reported live from outside the Jacksonville Sheriff's Office.

"I'm Kimberly Longview, reporting live where, early this morning, officers brought in Larry Long."

They posted a picture of Spank on the screen.

Tiger stared at the mugshot. "I seen that dude somewhere before," he whispered, careful not to wake Cookie.

"Mr. Long was brought in on a misdemeanor possession charge. While in custody, a warrant appeared for his questioning in the murder of Officer Phillip Shephard. According to reports, Long's sister admitted to letting her brother use her car the day before to run errands. Long is not being charged at this time—police are following up on all leads and suspects. They are also looking to question this man..."

A photo of Taz flashed on-screen.

"Trevor McMillan. He, too, may have information that could help bring this case to a close and give the Shephard family justice."

Tiger laid back, wrecking his brain. *Taz? In this mess?* And where the hell had he seen Spanky before? He rewound the last few days in his head—specifically that night at Lez's. Then it hit him.

He shot upright. "That was the nigga parked outside Lez apartment in that blue bubble Chevy!"

His thoughts darted to the convo at the hospital. Taz said he knew Lez had been shot—then switched it to, he heard she was shot. And then that line..."*The game's like chess, and you gotta be willing to sacrifice any piece. Even the queen.*"

Tiger's mind raced. What really happened the night he left Lez's? Why was that Larry dude sitting outside her apartment? And most importantly...Did Taz know something? Or worse— was he involved?

***

Later that night at Club Heavy, Tiger pulled up to the valet with Cookie in the passenger seat. Two valet attendants rushed to each side and opened their doors.

"Wzup, Mr. Tiger," one of them greeted. "Wassup, Craig," Tiger replied, slipping him a ten-dollar bill.

He grabbed the duffel bag from the backseat and circled around to catch up with Cookie.

"Still don't understand why you brought that big ole' bag," Cookie said, strolling down the carpet as they bypassed the line.

On the way to the entrance, several people shouted Tiger's name, giving him dap like he was a celebrity. Some he recognized.

Some he didn't. Didn't matter. He was just being hospitable. One guy in particular made it his business to make his presence known to Tiger. He brushed past the line, trailed by five of the sexiest chicks Tiger had ever seen.

Detective Holzendorf—undercover, dressed in civilian clothes.

"Whoa! Whoa! Whoa! Hold right here, big homie," Tyrone, the door bouncer, said as Holzendorf tried to skip the line.

Tiger, talking with the other bouncer Dre', caught the commotion just a few yards away. "What's the holdup, big man?" the detective said. "Me and my lady friends tryin' to get up in here and lock in a VIP spot before they all taken. So, what's the holdup?" He slung his arm around two of the women.

"You can't just skip these people like that!" Tyrone snapped. "They trying to get in,

just like you."

"Peep this, big homie," Holzendorf said, stepping closer to Tyrone like he was gonna whisper—but he made sure Tiger could hear.

"I flew these girls in from Miami... and I'm tryin' to show 'em a good time. Right here."

Tyrone gave him a blank stare.

"Well peep this then," the detective continued, peeling off several hundred-dollar bills from a thick knot. "How 'bout I pay a lil extra for you to look away, and we all be happy?" He patted Tyrone's shoulder. "What do ya say, big homie?" Tyrone shook his head.

"I understand you doing your job. But the manager around? Somebody I can talk to? I'm sure when he sees the girls I brought, he'll see things a lil more... my way."

Tyrone glanced back at Tiger. "Ya boy wanna holla at ya."

Holzendorf walked over and gave Tiger dap. "This yo place, big man?"

"It's a friend of mine... Wzup?" Tiger replied.

"As you can see, I'm tryin' to get me and my friends inside," he preached.

"I feel ya. But everybody tryin' to get inside. If you wanted VIP, you gotta call in advance, ya feel me?" Tiger explained.

"I feel ya, homie... but we here now, and the girls ready and willing." He stepped aside so the women could give a little preview of their exotic dance skills. "Now, you wouldn't send something like this to the back, now would ya? You should want this inside ASAP."

Tiger paused. Looked over at Dre' and slipped off the duffel bag.

"Run this upstairs to Heavy," he said. "Tell him I'll be up in a minute."

Then he turned to Cookie, who looked agitated. "Why don't you go grab our table," he told her. She sucked her teeth and walked off.

Turning back to Tyrone, Tiger nodded. "Go 'head and let him in. He good."

Tiger headed inside the club, when Det. Holzendorf called out, "Aye, Big homie"

Tiger turned to see who called him.

"Wanted to say, good looking out at the door" "You straight, homie" Tiger responded, as he was about to leave.

"I'm Domino" Holzendorf began.

"You what!" Tiger asked,

not really paying attention.

"I said, I'm Domino"

"Oh! Okay! Wzup?"

Tiger responded, not really caring.

"And this is Candy, Diamond, Mercedez, Chocolate, and Pocah"

That was the first thing Domino had said that had gotten Tigers attention. Even though he wanted to stay with Domino and the girls, he had things to do and people to see.

"No offense, big homie.. I gotta bounce"

He gave Domino some dap as he stated, "you and your company enjoy yaself. If ya need anything, gimme a holla" Tiger walked off.

Det. Holzendorf mumbled, "I'mma definitely give ya a holla. Best believe buddy, you will here from me again"

Tiger was on his way to the V.I.P. with Cookie when he got cut off.

"HEEEEY boo!"

Keisha ran up and threw her arms around his neck.

"**WHOOOA!**" Tiger roared, easing her off—nervous Cookie might be watching.

"**HEEEY**, you!"

"Keisha," she cut in, catching that he'd forgotten her name.

"Keeeiisha. Riiight... Wzup?"

He glanced up toward the V.I.P., spotting Cookie staring down at him.

"My homegirl's on the other side of the club. We been looking for you all night," Keisha said, dancing around him.

"I was gonna call you, but I didn't wanna seem too hard up. I'm really enjoying myself out here. We been—"

"Keisha," Tiger cut in. She was yapping. All he heard was blah, blah, blah.

He grabbed her shoulders, trying to calm her down.

"I gotta go say hey to some people," Tiger began "How 'bout you go over there with your friends, and I'll come by in a few with a bottle—maybe take y'all backstage to meet Rick Ross. What you think of that?"

"Oh my God! Really?" Keisha jumped up and down, still trying to hug on him. He kept playfully pushing her off with his arm. "Aahite, now! Leave before I change my mind." "Okay!... I'm going!... I'm gone!"

Tiger watched her fade into the crowd
before he moved.

"Project bitches," he joked. "Gotta love 'em.

Tiger flew upstairs to the V.I.P. where Cookie was waiting— arms crossed, attitude loaded.

"I seen ya entertaining ya lil girlfriend," Cookie began as Tiger sat down.

"Don't start that, Cookie. Please! That girl is a nobody!"

"She look like a somebody to me,"
she snapped back.

"WELL SHE AIN'T, okay!" Tiger fired, pushing her buttons even more.

"Baby, we're here to have a good time. Let's not argue, okay?" He grabbed Cookie's hands and kissed them—both of them. "What ya drinking?"
He asked, trying to de-escalate.

"Let's get a bottle, get wasted, go home, and break the head- board. You'd like that?"
Cookie smiled slightly, but didn't respond.

Before Tiger could stand, Dre—the door bouncer—came over with a bottle of Nuvo on ice and two champagne glasses.

"Who told you to bring this over here?" Tiger asked, scanning for Heavy or Pie Yay.

"Dude from earlier... with them five chicks," Dre said, then nodded toward the dance floor. "There he go, right there."
Tiger locked eyes with Detective Holzendorf—still undercover, still known to him as Domino.

Domino held up his bottle and nodded at Tiger. Tiger nodded

back.

"I never seen him before," Dre said.

"Bae, who is that?" Cookie asked, already opening the bottle.

"I don't know," Tiger replied, eyes locked on Domino as he danced with his crew of women. They looked like they were having the time of their lives. Something about the dude caught Tiger's attention. He hated meeting new people—especially strangers in his circle—but Domino had a vibe. He wasn't thirsty, didn't chase clout, and clearly had pull with the ladies. And from the looks of him? He gets money.

Detective Holzendorf had laid the bait, and Tiger bit.

"Go get him, Dre," Tiger said. "Ask him and his company to come join us."

He nodded toward Domino. "I wanna thank him for the drank."

Upstairs in the office, Heavy and Pie Yay had a perfect view of the club floor. Pie Yay was still searching for the five girls that had been dancing on each other earlier.

"Where the hell did they go?" he snapped, scanning the crowd. "I know they ain't dip yet."

Heavy helped scan the club., in search of Tiger. "There go Tiger big-head ass, over there," he pointed out.

Pie Yay followed his line of sight.

"There them hoes go I was talkin' 'bout, right there!" Pie snapped, hyped. "Tiger done snatched 'em up!"

"Daaamn, them hoes bad," Heavy added.

"Call that nigga phone," Pie said.

Tiger picked up as Pie told him to look up at the office. He glanced up, saw them acting wild. "Who them hoes you wit?" Pie asked.

Tiger could hear Heavy in the background yelling, "Bring 'em upstairs!"

Tiger laughed. "They wit some dude named Domino. I guess he they pimp or something." "Okay. Hell, that's even better," Pie said. "Line 'em up and bring 'em up here."

As bad as Tiger wanted to—especially with Mercedes massaging his meat under the table with her foot—Cookie was with him. And there was no way in hell he was moving anywhere without her welded to his hip. Domino was standing next to him as he was talking to Pie. "That one of ya homeboys calling bout the girls?" Holzendorf asked.

Tiger nodded, trying to play it cool so Cookie didn't catch on.

"Well, they got a price on they head," Domino smirked. "I hope they pockets deep, cause they not cheap. If they got a lil cash, they can get a lil a—"

"Alrighty, bruh," Tiger laughed, cutting him off.

He told Pie he'd be up in a minute and he ended the conversation.

"So you part owner of this place?" Domino asked, leaning on the balcony.

"Noooo! It's my homeboy spot," Tiger said, shaking his head. "Too much stress, dealing with all these different people. You got the DJ, bouncers, bartenders, and the doormen... Too many folks you gotta trust wit yo money."

"I feel ya, homie. So what do you do?" Domino asked, watching Tiger close.

There was a pause.

"A lil of this, a lil of that," Tiger finally said. Domino nodded, a slight grin spreading. "A lil of this, a lil of that, huh? I can dig it, homie."

Tiger laughed. "You trip me out how you talk. Sound like a real pimp with all that 'I can dig it' shit and all that rhyming earlier."

"Who's to say I'm not a pimp?" Domino replied, dead serious.

"Well, you sure got the right staff on ya team if you are," Tiger said, nodding at the women dancing all over each other.

"I'm not really a meet-new-people type of person," Tiger admitted.

"But you seem alright, Domino."

"I was thinking the same thing about you, big homie. Maybe we can hang out, hit the town one day."

Detective Holzendorf was in deeper than he planned—and faster than he planned.

"We can prolly make that happen,"

Tiger said, nodding.

"Well, I'mma let you and yo lady enjoy the rest of y'all night," Domino said, scanning the crowd.

"I think Rick Ross 'bout to come out anyway. I'mma try to get my girls on stage so they can do what they do."

They exchanged numbers, dap'd up, and they parted ways.

Cookie watched as Tiger programmed Domino's number into his phone.

"Oh, you can program his number in your phone, but not mine."

Tiger glanced up at Cookie, confused.

"I know your number by heart. I don't need to program it."

"Whatever, Tiger!" she snapped, no real comeback—just heat.

She slouched back in her chair, attitude heavy.

"I know you ain't gonna sit here and be petty about this!" he fired, standing up and walking to the balcony.

Cookie followed as the DJ started calling Rick Ross to the stage. She watched Tiger, trying to spark a reaction—but his eyes weren't on the show. She tracked his line of sight.

He was watching Domino's every move.

"I don't trust him," Cookie said suddenly, sharp enough to pull him back.

"What you say?" Tiger turned, eyebrows raised. "Your lil friend that just left from up here," she said, pointing down toward Detective Holzendorf.

"I don't know what it is about him. I just don't trust him."

Tiger turned his gaze back toward Domino. What's this dude really after,

other than the girls?

Tiger could pull women on his own.

This felt different. He saw something in Domino—same energy he caught from Heavy and Pie Yay when they first linked. Still, Cookie had never gotten a bad read on anyone Tiger moved with, business or personal. Then again, he thought. Nobody ever showed up flanked with five dime pieces, neither.

Rick Ross had the crowd jumping, and Domino even got his girls on stage. Cookie was tipsy and primed for some headboard breaking. Tiger was hot too—heated and buzzing. He figured he should holla at Heavy and Pie Yay before dipping. Leaving Cookie up in the VIP, he slid through the crowd. Halfway in, Keisha collided with him.

"**HEEEEEY BAAAABY!**" she slurred.

"I thought... I... I-I thought... I thought you were gonna... gonna take me. Us to see—" She paused, struggling for the name.

"Riss Rock! Ross Rick! Rick Ross!"

Tiger bit back a laugh, easing past her.

Lisa, Keisha's homegirl, staggered right into his path. She almost hit the floor.

"My girl... My... My girl Keisha... Keisha been looking for you **AAALLL** night long," she said, yanking him close to whisper.

"She um... She... She wanna... Umm... She want u to do it to her."

She giggled like a damn clown, then collapsed in Tiger's arms.

74

Right then, Pie Yay called.

"Who them new chicks you got with you?" he asked, yelling over the club noise.

"Just some head hunters I met earlier this week," Tiger replied, trying to keep Lisa upright.

"Bring them up. A.S.A.P." Pie ordered.

Tiger laughed and hung up. He motioned to Marlo and Bruce—two of the club bouncers—and had them escort Keisha and Lisa upstairs to Heavy's office.

He didn't even need to look back to know Cookie was clocking every move he made. When he looked up toward the V.I.P, it was clear Cookie was having her own problem. A dark-skinned dude with dreads was tugging on her, and Tiger could tell she was aggravated. He shot back up to the V.I.P. Dre clocked him running through the crowd and came up right behind.

"DON'T TOUCH ME AGAIN!" Cookie yelled.

"I Told You Nicely I Don't Wanna Dance!"

Tiger and Dre got upstairs just in time to stop the dude from doing something dumb enough to get hurt—or worse.

"Everything aahite up here?" Tiger asked, trying to give the guy an out.

"I'm aahite, Cuz!" he said, looking at Tiger while swaying on his feet.

"This bitch thinks she's God's gift!"

Tiger was about to snap when Cookie jumped in. "**BITCH! BITCH! I GOT YO BITCH**!" she shouted. Dre stood behind the dude, fists clenched, waiting on the go.

"My nigga! You may wanna bounce before you get smashed on for talkin' 'bout my girl like that," Tiger warned.

"My bad, big homie," the dude mumbled, still wobbling.

Tiger figured it was over—until the clown ran his mouth again.
"**YOUR BITCH!**" he said, loud and ignorant.
"Acts like she's God's gift."

Before he could spit another syllable, Tiger grabbed the Nuvo bottle off the table and cracked it across his head—laid him flat.

As the blood gushed from his face, Dre stomped him out without a word.

Tiger grabbed Cookie and led her out the club. "When you done," Tiger barked over his shoulder, "Throw his ass out."

8

The Three Takes

Tiger was at home with Cookie, getting a massage when the news came on. Another update on the officer murdered over on University Blvd.

Still no one in custody, according to reporter Kimberly Longview. She mentioned someone was wanted for questioning. Then the news flashed a picture of Taz on the screen.

Not long after, Tiger's phone rang.

"Hey Auntie," he said, still locked in on the TV. "Yeah, I see him... I'm watching it right now," he added, referring to Taz and the cop murder.

Ms. Kat wanted to know if Tiger thought Taz had anything to do with it.

"I doubt it. But when it comes to Taz,
it's hard to tell."

As they continued talking—reminiscing on the wild shit Taz used to pull back in the day—the screen cut to an Unsolved Mystery Crime Stoppers Bulletin. Outta nowhere, a photo of Ace lit up the screen. The report said his body had been found days ago, dumped in a ditch off 45th and Moncrief.

Tiger froze. He knew his aunt was watching the same broadcast.

"Auntie," he said calmly into the phone.

No answer.

"**AUNTIE!**" he shouted louder, panic now cracking through his voice. Tiger could hear her TV through the phone—so he knew she hadn't hung up.

"**I GOTTA GET TO MY AUNT HOUSE!**" he yelled, jumping out of bed.

"What happened?" Cookie called back, panicking.

"I don't know! One minute we were talking, then the news started talking 'bout Ace being dead and... and—"

"And what?" Cookie asked, her voice shaking.

"I don't know! Her phone just went silent. I could still hear the TV and everything in the background though."

Tiger threw on some clothes fast and bolted for the door.

"Call me when you find out suttin!" Cookie shouted as he rushed out.

Tiger pulled up in his aunt's yard in a full-blown panic. He almost tore the gear shift apart, throwing the truck in park while it was still rolling. He rushed to the door.

Locked.

He knocked. No answer. Checked the windows. Also locked.

Tiger yelled, banged, and did all he could to get his aunt's attention. Nothing.

His last resort—call the paramedics.

Within five minutes, the fire department and ambulance showed up. No hesitation. They knocked the door down.

Tiger rushed inside—and froze. His aunt was laid out on the hallway floor.

"Auntie!" he shouted, trying to run to her side, but someone held him back.

Her house phone was inches from her hand, buzzing loud.

"Is she okay?" Tiger asked, heart racing.

An officer tried tugging him again.

"Don't touch me!" he snapped.

"Sir, I need you to step out so they can work," the officer responded.

Tiger backed off as the paramedics got to work. They waved a capsule under her nose. Smelling salts. Instantly, she stirred. Tiger exhaled in relief as they questioned her, then prepped her for the gurney—to check for head trauma or internal injury.

From the stretcher, she cried out,

"Lord, Lord, Lord... Why, Lord? Why my baby?"

Tiger stepped closer, grabbed her hand.

"I'm here, Auntie."

She turned her head slowly, eyes locking on his—then snapped.

"Get thee behind me, **SATAN!**" she screamed, yanking away from him. "You did this!" she shouted, catching everyone's attention.

"YOU DID THIS! YOU DID IT!"

She kept yelling all the way to the ambulance. Tiger tried to follow, but an officer inside the house stepped in.

"Do you mind answering a few questions?" "About what!" Tiger snapped.

"About what happened here today."

Tiger turned, jaw tight,

ready for the back and forth.

"What's your name?"

The officer asked, notepad ready.

"Jerry," Tiger lied.

"Jerry what, sir?"

"Springer."

"Jerry Spr—"

The officer stopped, mid-writing, realizing.

"Sir, this is not a laughing matter. All I asked was basic information—and what happened here today"

"No. You asked who I was, which ain't got NOTHING to do with what went on here,"

Tiger snapped. "My aunt's headed to the hospital. That's my concern. How she got there? What happened?" He paused, then blurted, "Ride out there and see."

Tiger jumped in his truck and peeled off. He wanted to check on her—but deep down, he knew she might snap on him again. He couldn't take that. He decided Cookie would go in his place. After calling Cookie and updating her on everything, Six hit Tiger's line next.

"We need to meet. Now."

***

The streets were talking loud, and word had already made its way back to Detective Holzendorf—DJ was out on a bust bond, and his target was Tiger.

"I worked too hard and too long to let the state fuck this up, Holzendorf muttered. They always leave too much room for error. And I'll be damned if he weasels outta this one, if he's guilty".

He knew he had to find DJ before someone else did. If Tiger already knew DJ was a snitch, he'd be a body before sundown— if he wasn't already.

***

Big Lez had miraculously come out of her coma. She could tell she was in the hospital, but had no idea why or how she got there. Her body was sore as hell, worn down from surgery and being laid up for so long.

A nurse walked in to check her vitals and change her dressings. When she saw Lez's eyes open, she gasped.

"Oh my Lord! You up!" she said, smiling and walking toward the bed.

"What happened?" Lez asked, noticing the tubes, bandages, and machines.

"You really don't remember, sweetie?" the nurse replied, spraying Lez's wounds and gently removing the gauze.

"I... I remember..." Lez paused, digging for anything solid in her memory.

One name flashed.

She grabbed the nurse's hand and, with a startled look, blurted out—

"Where's Tiger?"

***

Tiger and Six pulled up to DJ's apartment in a rented Chevy Impala. The block was quiet—low activity, which was for the best.

"You absolutely sure that DJ... my DJ... workin' for them crackas?" Tiger asked, just as he hung up the phone after telling DJ he was outside "We'll see in a minute, won't we."

Tiger didn't wanna believe it. Of all the things he could call DJ, "snitch" wasn't supposed to be one of them. He leaned back in the seat, mind racing through all the shit that'd gone down lately. "That's the dude right there I saw at the station," Six said, pointing toward someone walking down the street.

Tiger sat up. His heart dropped.

It was DJ.

"So you one-hundred percent sure that's the guy you saw snitching?" Tiger asked again, still hoping for a different answer.

"I hate to be the bearer of bad news," Six said, eyes locked on DJ. "But that's one

of your roaches."

DJ waved for Tiger to come inside. Tiger was about to hop out when Six stopped him. "Remember—he workin' for them people. I told you I saw him get wired up... so be careful what you say," Six warned as they both stepped out. "He owe me some money anyway," Tiger said. "Once I get that... then it's whatever."

"Gotcha," Six replied, cracking a devilish smile.

***

Meanwhile, Detective Holzendorf was flying through traffic trying to get to Ken Knight. He was convinced DJ's days were numbered. He knew that once DJ's snitch status came out, Tiger wouldn't wait.

Holzendorf had already tried calling Tiger a few times, hoping to link up and keep him away from DJ. If DJ got killed, it could blow his whole investigation. Worse—it could send Tiger into hiding for years.

Then again, he thought, *Tiger's gonna need a new go-to guy. And maybe... just maybe... he'll even admit to killing DJ, to make an example outta what he do to snitches. Then I got him for murder too.* Holzendorf smirked.

This could work out for the best.

But the thought wouldn't stop spiraling—*If I take DJ into custody, Tiger'll still need a new runner...*He realized at this point—he really didn't need DJ anymore. DJ had been just a knight, used to try and keep the king in check. Holzendorf didn't want another Black-on-Black death on his conscience, and whatever he had to do to stop it—he would.

Speeding through traffic, he muttered, "I just hope Tiger haven't heard the rumor about DJ being an informant, or he's fucked."

***

"You got them couple dollars you owe me?" Tiger asked as soon as they walked inside.

"Yeah! Yeah! I gotcha." DJ answered,

nervous as hell.

"Well go get it."

Tiger said after DJ just stood there.

"Oh. Yeah... okay."

Tiger and Six watched as DJ hurried into the back room to grab Tiger's money.

"What ya think?" Tiger whispered to Six.

"Ya boy hotter than a fire cracka," Six said, staying ready.

"I know," Tiger admitted. He already knew what had to be done.

Tiger was about to say more,

but Six raised a finger.

"Shhh. You hear that?"

Tiger shook his head. "No."

"He talkin' to somebody," Six added.

He pulled his pistol,

kept it low behind his back—ready.

Moments later, DJ came out holding a brown bag with Tiger's money.

He shut the door behind him.

"Here ya go," DJ said.

"Somebody here wit you?" Tiger asked, grabbing the bag and checking inside.

"Nah!" DJ snapped quickly. "It's just us."

Tiger clocked DJ's antsy movements. He and Six exchanged a look—.

both reaching the same conclusion.

"Ima need five more brick in about an hour," DJ said, sweat creeping down his face.

"Five bricks, huh?" Tiger replied, nonchalant. "What happened to—"

Before he could finish, Six cleared his throat, a sharp reminder to keep it short.

There was a dead silence.

"This shit you got now, that's that butter... straight scale," DJ pushed on,

fishing for a response.

Tiger stayed quiet.

"You must've gotten that shit straight from Colombia, huh?" DJ joked weakly.

Still nothing.

"It's about that time, ain't it?"

Six asked, clutching his pistol.

"Just about," Tiger replied, eyes locked on DJ."Y'all bout to dip?"

DJ asked, trying to ease the tension.

"Yeah," Tiger said. "I think we're done here."

He glanced at Six. "You agree?"

"Oh absolutely," Six grinned, devilish.

"There's *nothing* else left for us here."

Tiger secured the bag of money and turned to leave. Six didn't move. He and Tiger locked eyes. "May I?" Six asked, ready to go.

Tiger took a long breath, gave DJ one last look, then turned to Six.

With a Heavy heart, he nodded.

"Handle ya business," Tiger said as he stepped toward the door.

DJ felt the shift, but before he could speak, Six raised the pistol and put one clean bullet through DJ's forehead.

Tiger couldn't bring himself to look. Hand on the doorknob, he paused.

"Don't forget to remove the wire," he said, stepping out.

Det. Holzendorf turned onto Ken Knight and floored the gas, racing to reach DJ. Tiger and Six were in the car, just about to pull off, when he pulled up. The tint on the rental was too dark for the detective to see inside—but Tiger saw him clear as day. "What's he doing here?" Tiger said as Six eased them off the curb. He thought about saying something to the detective—but if Domino was headed to DJ's apartment and found that body, Tiger didn't want to be the last man seen walking out. "You get the wire?" Tiger asked, eyeing Six. After a pause, Six replied, "He wasn't wearing one."

Tiger's eyes snapped wide. "What the hell you mean he wasn't wearing one?" he barked. "He wasn't.??

"YOU FUCKIN TOLD ME YOU SAW HIM GETTING A WIRE PUT ON HIM!" Tiger snapped, shaking his head in disbelief.

"I did," Six said, still calm.

"What the fuck!" Tiger growled.

"So what was the point of that shit back there "That was exactly what I said it was,"

Six said coolly. "Ya boy was snitchin'. Ya heard me. Bottom line."

Tiger clenched the wheel, mind spinning. "He prolly was gonna wait til you double back wit them five bricks," Six added. Tiger replayed the scene in his head. It kinda made sense. But one thing still didn't sit right—how did DJ know Domino, when just days ago he claimed he didn't have a connect down here?

Six didn't help ease it.

"Nowadays, whoadie, nobody's who they say they are. Everybody got snitch tendencies. I wouldn't be surprised if there's a couple more just like that... waiting for the three Takes—either take yo spot, take you out, or take you down."

Tiger listened, silent.

"You only gotta focus on one Take, if they try ya," Six said, voice flat.

"And that's to take them out."

9

Pest Control

Early the next morning, Tiger got a surprising call from Ice.
"I hear you got a lil roach infestation that needs exterminatin'," Ice said, referring to the incident where Tiger lost the money and dope.
"How the hell you know 'bout it?"
Tiger asked, shocked.
"I make it my business to know damn near everything that moves in these streets—especially when it involves people I deal with."
"I take that as a good thing," Tiger replied.
"Ya damn right it is," Ice confirmed. "I got people in high places."
"That's wzup," Tiger said, sounding relieved.
"So, how you handlin' this?" Ice pressed.
"I got people on it... if that's what you askin'," Tiger said.
"What you mean, you got people on it? What they done so far?"
  Tiger paused, but said nothing.
"Just like I thought," Ice cut in. "How 'bout I send my personal exterminator down to handle it? He'll have you pest-free in no

time."

"That'll work," Tiger said. "Who is he, and when he comin'?"

"His name's Six. He from New Orleans. He'll be in touch with the details."

"That's a bet," Tiger agreed.

Before hanging up, Ice added: "You focus on the money. Let me handle the war."

***

"Daaaamn!" Taz said, eyeing Champ's swollen face. "You been beat up and beat down!"

Spank and Champ laughed as they inspected the damage.

"Get ya laughs out now!" Champ snapped, pissed. "Shit ain't gon' be funny when I go back to Club Heavy and blow that bitch up."

"The club ain't do that to yo face," Taz smirked. "Some niggas in the club did that,"

Champ clarified.

"A nigga fist did that," Spank cut in.

"Nah!" Taz jumped back in. "A mule hoof did that shit!"

"Fuck both of y'all," Champ barked. "I told you, the nigga hit me wit a bottle."

"Who? You see the nigga face?" Spank asked "That's a dumb ass question... of course I seen the nigga face!"

"That was a legitimate question,"

Spank shrugged. "You apparently ain't see the nigga fist."

Taz and Spank cracked up again.

"Like I said," Champ growled, "if I ever see that nigga again, I'mma kill him and that bitch he was with!"

"This time, if you fight," Spank added, trying not to laugh, "do me a favor—make sure you don't hit his fist wit yo eye no mo'."

88

***

Tiger went by the hospital to visit Big Lez. She was still in recovery, and the doctor said she was in a temporary coma. He allowed Tiger to see her for a brief moment, mentioning that hearing familiar voices of loved ones sometimes helps. Tiger walked into Lez's room and couldn't bear the sight. She lay in the bed, almost lifeless, hospital sheets pulled to her chest, tubes and IVs in her arms. He moved slowly from the foot of the bed to her face, leaned in, and placed his hand on her stomach with a light sigh.

"Doc say you were eight weeks pregnant with twins," Tiger said, heavy-hearted. He paused, then eased in closer.

"Were they mine?" he asked with a painful smile. "Would I have been a father? Of twins?" The thought alone was remarkable to him.

"It woulda been funny seeing you pregnant," Tiger chuckled. "You waddling around fat and bitchy." He paused.

"Well, you always been bitchy."

For all the chaos she carried, she looked peaceful—quiet, angelic. He leaned in and kissed her forehead.

"You woulda made a wonderful mother," he said, trying to shake off a tear. "I'm so sorry 'bout this, Lez!" he continued. "This is all my fault! I did a real shitty job of keeping you safe."

Tiger took another deep breath.

"I'm so used to you being so tough actin', that I let the outer shell block my reality—that you a delicate, afraid little girl."

He rubbed her arm, voice low and steady.

"Just know that I will not rest until everyone involved are in matching coffins."

***

Detective Holzendorf was getting real comfortable with the

progress he was making with Tiger. He just needed Tiger to open the door—to show him a glimpse of his world on the dope side. But Tiger wasn't about to volunteer that part of his life. So Holzendorf cooked up a plan. He called in a couple favors from agency contacts. The play was simple: bring Tiger along to witness him "buying" weight from another undercover posing as a plug. Holzendorf wanted Tiger to believe he too could do a lil of this, a lil of that.

***

When Tiger left the hospital, his phone rang. It was Heavy. "Wzup my boy?" Heavy said, sounding hyped. "I'm chillin! Wzup wit you?" Tiger replied.

"I just called to say, good lookin out on them breezies you sent up to the office last night," Heavy started. "They were some real meat monsters... And that Keisha chic," he added, excited.

"Whaaat!" Tiger cut in. "I heard she had a mean head game."

"She'll give SupaHead a run for her money," Heavy bragged. "And her lil buddy? She rode Pie Yay like she was in a rodeo."

"Daaaamn! I missed all that?" Tiger asked.

"Yep! But the good part about it is, I'm living it again right now."

"They over there right now?" Tiger jumped in. "Nah, even better," Heavy said proudly.

"I taped it."

After Tiger got off the phone with Heavy, another unexpected call came in—this time from Det. Holzendorf.

"I was wondering how ya schedule
look for this evening?"

"I aint got too much going on... Wzup?"
Tiger asked.

"Wanted to know if you didn't mind ridin wit me somewhere?"

Tiger didn't know this man from Adam, and he made that clear. "Nah, it ain't nothing like that, bruh," the detective defended. "I just gotta go holla at a partna of mine. Then I gotta go snatch up a couple mo girls."

That last part caught Tiger's attention.

"Plus I wanted to holla at you about... how can I say this?" He paused, then blurted, "A lil of this, a lil of that."

Tiger was on his way back home when a number popped up in his phone that he ain't never seen before.

"Who dis?" he asked, wondering who was calling his personal line.

It was Six—Ices' personal hitman outta New Orleans. He told Tiger he was in Jacksonville, and he'd hit him back once he got situated to go over the details of the job. Tiger felt a whole lot better about the situation now. Whoever took his money was about to become an example. Their death would speak loud and clear: Whatever you thinking... Don't do it.

Later that evening, Tiger met up with Det. Holzendorf at Wal-Mart. Even though him and the Detective had been getting cool, Tiger still ain't know him like that. And Holzendorf was doing everything in his power to change that. Domino had this whole fake drug deal set up and ready to roll. He and two other agents staged a deal—posing as Miami boys pushing weight. Domino was supposed to buy two kilos at a jacked-up price.

The whole play? Get Tiger to bite.

If Tiger saw that kind of money moving, maybe he'd want to cut out the middleman and sell straight to Domino. And once that happened, boom—hand-to-hand to an undercover. The charge Holzendorf needed to bury Tiger for a long time.

Domino and Tiger pulled up at the Marriott. Tiger felt a twist in his stomach—this setup had him shook. Domino caught his look and told him to chill, saying he was the only one with something to lose and Tiger was just there to make it look even.

"How long you been dealing wit these cats?" Tiger asked, scanning the lobby.

"A lil over eight months," Domino said. "I used to stay in Ft. Myers some years ago. I got caught up and did five years up fed. When I got out, moved down here—been here two years now." They stepped inside and headed to the elevator. "I deal wit these dudes 'cause my cousin used to deal with them before he was killed."

"How ya cousin got killed?" Tiger asked as the doors dinged on the fourth floor.

Domino paused, hunting for a clean answer. A few steps later, he knocked on the room's door and finally said,

"He was killed in a robbery."

"Wzup Domino?" one of the detectives, who called himself Tree, stated.

"I can't call it," Domino responded, as he gave him dap and they walked inside.

Tiger looked around at their surroundings to make sure there'd be no more surprises. He watched as Domino gave dap to another guy who was known as Marlo. They both were clean shaven, Coogi fitted with white Air Force Ones. Basic watches, no golds, no earrings—not as much as a fitted chain. Their speech was proper, their slang was raggedy, and Tiger noticed they talked as if they were Yale graduates. There was no swagger about them to convince Tiger they were big-time suppliers from Miami. If they were from Jacksonville, they'd get robbed every day, Tiger thought.

"**Tiger!**" Domino called to him. "What you think about this?"

92

Marlo opened a small bag and pulled out two kilos. Both were in individual sandwich bags.

"It is what it is, man," Tiger spoke,

not feeling comfortable.

"It is what it is? What's that mean?" Tree asked, staring at Tiger.

Tiger gave him a crazy return look.

These niggas can't be that green, he thought to himself. Domino opened the bag and smelled the fragrance. "This that shit, huh?" he looked up and asked Tiger.

Marlo egged Tiger to check out their product. "Let me holla at ya a minute!" Tiger stated to Domino as he headed to the door.

Outside, Tiger blurted, "Either this a set-up and we about to get robbed, or ya boys the police." "What gives you that assumption?"

Domino him asked nervously.

He wondered if Tiger really peeped something, or was just nervously uncomfortable.

"It's too many things they doing

that says police!"

"**LIKE WHAT?**" Domino asked,

trying to act shocked.

"They too clean cut for one. They don't got no swagger about themselves. And the worst part is, they too comfortable. They chillin' like they don't got two bricks on 'em."

Domino smiled for a moment. "Is that it?" He placed his hand on Tiger's shoulder and stated, "They cool people. I trust them and they trust me, it's cool"

"But they don't know me from a can of paint. And it's funny that not one of them asked me a question or gave me a second look,"

Tiger spoke seriously. "You really don't even know me," he stated to Domino. "I could be a jack-boy for all y'all know."

He's a lil smarter than he let off to be, Domino thought about Tiger. He had to be cautious about how he handled this situation,

or Tiger may walk.

"How 'bout this?" Domino started. "We go back in there and try to finish the deal... If you still feel uncomfortable, alert me, and we'll leave." Tiger shook his head at Domino. "You think they drove over five hours with two bricks, just to drive back with 'em? You paying for them bricks rather you want 'em or not!"

"Well what you expect me to do?" Domino asked, acting curious. "This is how I eat, and I don't know anybody else... I'm backed into a corner."

Tiger thought for a moment. Domino felt this plan was already turning out to be a success. Whether Tiger knew it or not, he'd trapped himself. He broke through the trust barrier between connect and client. Tiger was on a whole other level of thinking. He felt he was risking his life and freedom for a guy he really didn't know anything about.

"How much are you even paying for these things anyway?" Tiger asked.

"Twenty-eight."

"**EACH?!**" Tiger snapped, just as Marlo opened the door.

"Everything okay out here?" Marlo asked. "Everything's Gucci," Domino confirmed.

"Well you might wanna come back inside. I don't wanna bring too much heat to this room."

Domino took a few steps toward the door then turned to face Tiger. Tiger thought hard for a moment. What did he really have to gain from this whole ordeal? Domino was about to pay fifty-six stacks for two keys. Still, Tiger couldn't shake that uncomfortable feeling about the Miami boys. Something was off. But even though he wasn't ready to let Domino buy from him just yet, he also wasn't feeling this current setup either.

"Everything is Gucci, right?" Domino asked again, watching him close.

Tiger glanced over at Domino, then to Marlo—and with a heavy sigh, he stated, "Yeah! Everythangs Gucci."

***

Six had already started his job—flushing out the corruption in Tiger's organization. Almost instantly, he found a roach. He was posted up at the police station, where an old buddy of his worked.

"What brings you on my side of the globe?" Sgt. Turner asked, giving Six some dap.

"Money," Six replied, dropping onto the edge of a desk.

"You chasing a bounty, huh?" Turner said, flipping through folders.

"Suttin like that," Six answered, eyes sharp.

"Oh, I know that look," Turner said with a smirk. "So what part do I play in this?"

Six broke it down. Most of the situation—just enough. The robbery. The money. That it all belonged to Ice. Sgt. Turner froze for a second. He'd heard Tiger's name around the precinct recently. Hell, he was pretty sure someone was already working an angle to bring Tiger down.

The two of them made their way down the hall to the private interrogation rooms. As luck would have it, the informant was inside—getting briefed on what the agency was calling

95

"Operation Tiger's Den."

"Who is that?" Six asked, locking in on the C.I."His name's Demarkus Jakes... On the streets, he go by DJ," Turner replied. Six watched through the one-way glass as two officers ran DJ through the playbook—

handing him wire equipment, walking him through his task.

"He was brought in a couple days ago. Three counts of trafficking. Possession of a firearm by a felon. Resisting with violence," Turner said, eyes on the file.

"The lil nigga was doing his thang on the streets. Caught with ten keys and five choppers. Lucky for us the guns weren't loaded. 'Cause I swear, the way he was fighting, he woulda laid out any cop that stepped up."

"So I guess he supposed to be some kinda Billy Bad Ass, huh?"

"I wouldn't say that," Turner answered. "He knew his record was toast. If they locked him, he'd be looking at life. He's a three-time loser—all for trafficking. That makes him an habitual traffic offender. Bottom line—he's fucked. Had no other choice but to snitch."

Six narrowed his eyes, watching DJ get strapped up with a wire.

"So the lil nigga ain't want no lawyer?" he asked."Yeah, he got one. One of the best. But at this point, all his lawyer can do is keep the needle out his arm," Turner replied.

They both shook their heads.

"That's just like a nigga," Six muttered. "When everything's good, he good. But best believe—when he's caught, everybody's caught."

10

Weight of the Crown

Six dropped Tiger at his truck, and Tiger decided to drive home. His week was crashing down before his eyes. So far he'd lost three hundred thousand dollars and five kilos. His cousin Ace was dead, his aunt and Big Lez were in the hospital, and now one of his closest friends and his best worker was dead too. *Could his life get any worse?* He thought to himself.

Pulling into his yard, he saw Cookie was home. He really needed her right now. Inside his room, she was sprawled out in bed, napping. He just wanted a hot shower and to lay down—to get this damn day behind him, He turned the TV on low, careful not to wake her.

"It seems that murders are on the rise..."

he murmured, watching footage of last night's killing outside Club Plush.

Kimberly Longview was on-site for the report.

After what started as a nightclub brawl turned into a shootout, three people were shot—one dead. JSO hadn't released names yet, but according to Kimberly Longview, it popped off when a young boy caught his ex-girl slow grinding with an alleged neighborhood rival. The cameraman panned the front of Club Plush as she wrapped up her segment:

"Suspects are still at large."

"Shit's getting crazy," Tiger muttered, nodding his head.

He stepped into the bathroom, started the shower, then came back out to grab some clothes just as Kimberly continued.

"The state may have a witness and video tape to help solve the murder investigation

of Officer Shephard."

Tiger's eyes shot wide. He was sure they were about to throw Taz's face on screen.

"News at eleven," she said,

just before it cut to the weather.

"NEWS AT ELEVEN?" Tiger snapped, looking at the clock—6:15 p.m.

"I'mma prolly be damnit sleep."

Tiger stepped into the hot shower, hoping to wash off the weight of the week. He let the water run down his back—until he felt a hand slide gently across his skin.

"I thought you were sleep," he mumbled, as Cookie's fingers moved up to his shoulders.

"I was," she whispered, kissing the center of his back. "I heard the shower on, and all of a sudden I felt... dirty."

Tiger turned around. She saw he was already at full attention. She took him in her hand, stroking slow under the heat.

That mix—her grip and the water— sent chills through his spine. Her body glistened in the steam and low light.

Tiger kissed her lips, then her neck, then down to her breasts. Her nipples were hard, and he gave them attention. His tongue moved over every inch of her as she caressed the top of his head, guiding him lower. He flipped his tongue over her

navel, teasing, before throwing her leg over his shoulder and diving in. She gasped as his tongue worked her, her body trembling. She gripped her breasts tight, moaning. When the waves hit, she reached for anything—his ears, the wall, air—thrusting forward to take every bit of the orgasm. "Yeeeeees!" she screamed,
shaking as her body peaked.

Tiger lifted up, mouth wet from the mix of juices and shower water. Cookie stared at him—breathless, eyes full of heat. Her legs were barely holding her up. He gripped her thighs, wrapped them around his waist, and adjusted his manhood. Slowly, he eased her down on it. She clawed his back lightly as he slid deeper inside. The hot water beating down on their bodies only intensified the fire between them.

He started to bounce her—slow, then faster. Cookie moaned, meeting every thrust. Tiger's legs burned, but he kept going. Then, he shifted. Eased her down, turned her around, bent her over, and lifted one leg onto the tub edge. She started to rise into him, but he grabbed her head and pushed it back down. Her leg shook. He gripped tighter and slammed deeper—
harder, faster.

"Baby! Baby! Baby!" she screamed, yanking the shower curtain off its hooks.
He couldn't hold back. Between the heat, the water, her soaked grip—he exploded inside her. Exhausted and satisfied, they rinsed off and crashed, tangled in each other's arms.

***

Detective Holzendorf sat in his car, pissed, watching the forensics team sweep through DJ's apartment. He knew his case was hanging by a thread now. DJ was their inside man—

wired up and working to bring down Tiger. And now DJ was dead. JSO would take this one personal.

"All that surveillance. All that work, down the fuckin' tube!" he snapped, slamming his fist against the steering wheel.

It seemed like the whole neighborhood came out when the coroner showed up. DJ's death was a big deal in that area. He supplied a lot of people, so now the title for the next neighborhood king was up for grabs.

Detective Holzendorf knew he was risking his cover hanging around the police like that. Any questions he needed to ask—or answer—would have to be done at the station.

He left his card with one of the officers to call if they needed anything or found something. The only information Det. Holzendorf gave the state investigators was that a grey 2010 or later model Chevy Impala with dark tint left the scene minutes before he realized DJ was dead.

He let them know he couldn't stick around to help, since he was undercover and didn't want to compromise his identity. Now, all he could do was let the state police hunt for the grey Impala, while he focused on finishing what he knew they couldn't. And that was wrapping up Operation Tiger's Den... his way.

***

Big Lez was discharged early the next morning. Her body was sore, her arm in a sling, and her mind still foggy from the night she was attacked. She lay in bed, tears in her eyes, replaying what the doctor told her about the babies. Through all the pain, all she could think about was Tiger—and whether he was okay. She wiped her tears, rubbed her stomach, looked up to Heaven and whispered, "Mommie's sorry." The tears kept coming. "Mommie's sooo... so sorry."

***

Taz woke up still tipsy from last night. He, Spank, and Champ had hit Mascara's Gentleman Club and balled out—throwing money like it was fresh off the government press, popping bottles like they'd won the championship.

Taz looked over and saw two naked girls in his bed, sleep, holding each other. He couldn't, to save his life, remember what happened last night—let alone how he got back to the spot.

He got up and walked through the apartment. Peeking in one room, he saw Spank still knocked out, a naked girl curled up with him. Taz noticed a half ounce of hydro, a wad of cash, and Spank's diamond bracelet sitting on the dresser.

"Dumb ass boy," Taz mumbled, walking in and sliding all the stuff into the top drawer of Spank's broken dresser.

"What time is it, bruh?" Spank asked groggily.

"I have no idea," Taz said, looking around. "Where's my shit!" Spank snapped, seeing the empty dresser.

He spun toward the girl beside him and barked, "BITCH, GET UP!! YOU GOT MY SHIT!"

"I put it in the top drawer," Taz cut in, eyeing the naked chick sprawled out, legs wide open.

She was so wasted off alcohol and ecstasy, she opened her eyes for a second, then passed right back out.

"What the hell happened last night?" Taz asked, rubbing his forehead.

With a grin, Spank said,

"Booooy, we had a ball last night."

Taz cracked a slight smile as

Spank kept going.

"We shut the club DOWN!! And you—"

He pointed at Taz.

"You were tore the fuck up...

all on the stage and er'thang."

"Well, how we got dem hoes?"

"You got 'em," Spank cut in. "You started snatching hoes off stage and all."

"Damn! And I don't remember none of that shit," Taz said.

"What happened to them two chicks you took in the room wit you last night?" Spank asked, leaning over to caress the girl's breast.

"They still in there," Taz said. "I just didn't know how they got there."

"Does it matter? Them broads were stupid fine," Spank added, hype.

"Plus, I came to check on y'all."

"Well, like I said, you got the girls and we're fine... so get out."

Spank climbed on top of the dancer, pulling the cover over them for some privacy. Taz waited a second, listening for sex sounds.

"Geeeet Ouuuut," Spank joked, realizing Taz never left.

He was headed to his room where he had two girls of his own— but decided to check on Champ first. As he got closer to Champ's room, he heard moaning and heavy breathing. The door was already cracked, so Taz nudged it just enough to peek inside. Champ had two girls too.

One was on her back, legs spread. The other was arched up in doggy style, face buried deep in the first girl's wetness—while Champ was behind her, humping like a jack rabbit.

Taz let out a light chuckle, just loud enough to catch Champ's attention. Champ looked back, saw Taz through the door, and waved for him to come help out with both girls. Taz shook his head no, and walked off—back to his own room, where his two girls were waiting.

When he stepped into his room, both girls were wide awake—already warming up without him.

"There he is," the bright red, naked girl said. "Yeah! Here I am," Taz replied, grinning as he climbed into bed with them.

"I reeeeally enjoyed last night," the slim, brown-skinned girl said, tugging at Taz's clothes again. "You did, huh?"

Taz didn't remember a damn thing from the night before—but he planned on re-enacting every second of it.

"I wanna do everything we did last night,"

he said, licking his lips as he took in both of their bodies.

"Everything?!?" they said in unison. "EVERYTHING,"

Taz confirmed, trying to sound seductive. "Sure," the red girl said, reaching into her purse and pulling out a ten-inch dildo.

"Daaamn!" Taz said, caught off guard. "Which one of y'all took all that?"

Both girls looked at each other, grinning, then turned to Taz and said—

"You did."

11

Family Ties, Blood Lies

Ace's funeral was held Saturday morning. Tiger covered all the arrangements. Ace was laid out in all white — his favorite white fur Kangol, white Cazelle clear-tint shades trimmed in diamonds (originally Tiger's, but Ace loved them). The casket was pearl white with gold trim, and the room smelled of white roses. A slide show played Ace's best moments throughout the service.

Cookie sat in the front row, holding Ace's daughter Tamela, doing her best to console Ms. Kat. Big Lez was next to them, and Tamika — Ace's baby mama — was trying to help. But every move she made just dug the hole deeper. Tamika leaned in front of Ms. Kat, arms spread "I'm so sorry about what happened to Ace, Ms. Kat," she said, reaching in for a hug.

"If you don't get out my face, I'mma snatch that dirty weave out yo head!" Ms. Kat snapped in a low, mean voice.

Tamika stepped back, teary-eyed and in shock. Ms. Kat locked eyes with her. There was heat behind every word.

"Chile... if I get up from this chair—"

Tamika froze until Cookie stood up beside her "Could you please

keep moving?
You see she upset," Cookie said.
Tamika looked at Cookie,
then at Tamela in her arms.
"Come to momma," Tamika said, as she reached for Tamela.
"That did it!" Ms. Kat snapped, jumping up and lunging toward Tamika.
Several family members—and even the usher—had to step in to break it up.

Tiger was on the third floor, watching the whole thing.
"Ghetto," he mumbled, shaking his head.
After the service, Tiger volunteered to be a pallbearer. He felt disgusted... and obligated. As he walked, he imagined hearing Ace's voice from inside the casket.
"Why, cuz! Why!"

At the burial site, the rest of the family followed to pay their last respects before Ace was lowered into his final resting place. Ms. Kat did her best to hold it together. On each side of her stood Tiger's two favorite women—Cookie and Big Lez.

With her good arm, Lez fanned Ms. Kat as she rocked back and forth, holding back tears. During the pastor's final words, Tiger's phone started ringing. He was about to ignore it—until he saw it was Six. He eased over by a tree, away from the family, and answered.

"Wassup, man? I'm at my cousin's funeral."
Six told him he found out who was behind robbing the spot.
"**BET!**" Tiger snapped, instantly alert.
"So how you want me to handle this?"
Six asked calmly.
"I want 'em dead,"
Tiger said, voice low and sharp.

"But first—I want you to torture they ass."

"You sure?"

"Damn right I'm sure. I ain't never been more sure about anything in my life."

"Alright then... consider it done," Six replied.

"But before you kill the head nigga,"

Tiger added, "I wanna look in his eyes. I wanna be the last thing he sees before he burns in hell."

Tiger hung up just as Taz walked up.

"You heard anything in the streets about who did this to cuz?"

"Why?" Tiger cut in.

"You gonna rob 'em or somethin'?"

"It's better than bein' soft and doin' nothin'!" Taz shot back.

"I had enough of that soft shit."

"And I had enough of that robbery shit,"

Tiger fired back.

"It ain't like I ever robbed you," Taz said.

"You robbed our connect before. That was like robbin' me... Hell, that was like robbin' us!"

He pointed between them.

"Bruh, that was like a hunnit years ago!"

Taz argued. "You ever gon' live that down?"

Tiger paused, thinking. Was what happened back then really that deep to still hold onto? He'd moved on. Found a better connect. Could he let that shit go? He always believed blood was thicker than water. But Ace's death—that made shit complicated.

"We're brothers, for Christ's sake,"

Taz said, waiting for a response.

Then, "You right," Tiger chimed in,

reaching out his hand.

"You damn right I'm right," Taz replied, pulling him in for a hug.

Tiger tried to hold back a tear.

"A'ight, nigga—enough of all that male love stuff," he joked.

Taz started to walk off as the funeral crowd began to disperse.

Tiger playfully slapped him on the butt.

"Great to have ya back," he said.

Taz grabbed his butt with a pained look.

"Try not to do that," he said. "My ass still hurtin' from an accident the other day."

***

Detective Holzendorf called Tiger later that evening. He wanted to give him condolences on the death of his cousin.

"Yall know who did it?" He asked being nosey. "Nah"

Tiger spoke. "And I doubt if they will either" "Why you say that?" Det. Asked.

"They only care bout they own" Tiger began. "You see they don't know who killed my cousin, them boys at the club the other day, or Dj... Yet, they got witnesses and a videotape for that cop.

Det. Holzendorf wanted Tiger to discuss all he knew about Dj and his death without saying he knew Dj.

"Who is Dj?" The Detective asked.

Tiger stared at him for a moment confused.

He was one-hundred percent sure that was domino he saw the night of Dj's murder. Tiger was so disoriented that he didn't wanna press the issue. He felt if Domino could play dumb, then so would he.

"Dj was just a petty lil neighborhood dope boy... You know, the kind the cops give two flying fucks bout"

107

Detective Holzendorf switched gears. Now he had to figure out a way to get Tiger to talk—about drugs, about supplying him.

Domino already knew the angle. But he also knew Tiger wouldn't say shit over the phone.

"I need to talk to you about something pretty important," Domino started.

"Wassup!" Tiger asked.

"Can I be blunt?"

"Not if you can help it," Tiger cut in fast.

Domino paused, then went for it.

"My buddies from the M.I. Yayo—they gonna be chillin' for a lil minute, and I may need
a new... friend."

"I may know somebody," Tiger said, sounding slightly convinced Domino might be straight. Tiger knew when an undercover talks, the convo had to be clean and clear.

"Let me look into something and
get back witcha."

"Sooner than later, I hope," Domino said"

"You never can tell, Mr. Domino... you never can tell," Tiger replied.

***

It had been a couple days since Big Lez got out the hospital. Every night since, she woke up in cold sweats—reliving the night she was attacked. Each nightmare ended the same: Taz in a devil suit, gun to her babies' heads. Every time she tried to save them, he pulled the trigger. She couldn't remember everything from that night—but one thing she knew for sure: Taz shot her. Taz killed her babies.

She saw him at the burial, talking with Tiger. And when she saw

108

them hugged up, her whole body went cold.

Tiger can't know Taz was the one that put me in that hospital, she thought. I wonder if he even knew I was pregnant with his babies.

She knew she couldn't tell Tiger—not yet. This one... she'd have to handle alone. Quietly.

***

Taz was headed back to the Southside—unaware he was being followed. He was feeling good, knowing he and Tiger were talking again. His only fear? Big Lez. He wondered if she'd ever tell Tiger what really happened. He saw her at the burial, but she didn't act like she remembered anything from that night. Life was good, he thought.

He stopped by the liquor store before linking up with Spank and Champ at the apartment.

He'd gotten Tiger's number at the funeral and figured now was as good a time as any to reach out. He called and invited him out—his treat. Tiger agreed. They planned to hit the town that night. Taz wanted to show Tiger he'd leveled up.

He pulled into the complex, still not knowing the he was being watched. He parked in front of his building, while the car trailing him stopped one building down—close enough to keep eyes on his door. Inside that car, the person checked their clip, made sure the bullets were loaded, and waited to see which apartment Taz went into.

Meanwhile, Tiger had been trying to call Lez, but she wasn't picking up. He hadn't seen her since she got discharged. He meant to talk to her at the burial, but by the time he finished with Taz, she was gone. Frustrated, he hung up—and his phone rang again. It was Six.

"I got the roaches here wit me," Six said.

"What you want me to do wit 'em?"

"How many is it?" Tiger asked, with a devilish smile creeping in.

"Three."

"Where you at?"

Tiger jumped in his truck and peeled off to the Southside.

"Have a lil fun wit 'em 'til I get there," he said. "But remember— don't squash the main roach.

I wanna be the last thang he see."

"I got all that," Six said.

"So what to do wit the other two?"

Tiger didn't even hesitate.

"FUCK 'EM."

***

Big Lez finally decided to call Tiger.

He answered before the first ring even finished "Wzup, ma?" he said.

"Nuttin, pa," she replied.

It had been a minute since they called each other that—it was their little Ghetto Puerto Rican talk. "Where ya at, daddy?" she said, laying on the charm.

"Just ridin'... Wzup?"

He didn't want her knowing the explicit details of his moves. But he did want to see her.

And like she read his mind, she asked—

"Can I see you tonight?"

BINGO, he thought, grinning.

Then he remembered—he'd told Taz they'd hang out tonight, and that mattered. But somehow, he had to fit Lez in.

"I got suttin to handle later on," he said.

"Can I swing through after that?"

"I guess so," she replied, as her voice dropped
a little.

"Just don't make me wait too long," she added, as they hung
up.

Tiger called Six and told him he was just down the street—
he'd be there in five minutes. "Well, well, well," Six muttered,
standing behind a battered and bruised Spank and Champ.
"I hate to bring this enjoyable moment to an end, fellas... but
like Nino Brown said in New Jack City—your services are no
longer needed in our community."

Six raised the pistols in each hand, aimed at the backs of their
heads, and pulled the triggers. Small bursts of brain matter shot
out the other side. Their bodies slumped on the couch, blood
oozing down into the cushions and pooling on the floor.

Six had Taz tied up and duct-taped to a chair in the kitchen,
forced to watch the whole ordeal. His face was swollen and
leaking—one eye nearly shut, lip busted, wheezing from too
many gut shots.

"The... mo—ney... in the room," Taz gasped out between ragged
breaths.

"Oh, this ain't about money, Cat Daddy," Six said, stepping
closer.

"Y'all get to be examples to the world."

He grabbed Taz's face, tilted it up so he had no choice but to
look him in the eye.

"Y'all fucked wit the wroooong nigga's money... and now you
get to use it to bury y'all ass."

He cracked Taz across the face—hard. Blood flew from his
mouth, spraying across the tile.

Tiger called Six and told him he was outside. Six gave him the
apartment number and told him the door was open.

"Don't pass out on me just yet, big guy," Six said, slapping Taz to wake him from unconsciousness. "The best is yet to come."
Six heard the front door open—had to be Tiger. "SIX!" Tiger shouted, spotting two bodies slumped on the living room sofa.
"I'M IN THE KITCHEN!" Six hollered back, standing behind Taz.
Tiger took a second to try to recognize the two John Does—but they were unidentifiable.
"Wake up, nigga!"
Six barked, slapping Taz again. "You gonna get plenty of rest in just one second."
    Tiger could hear the chaos from the kitchen—blows landing, groans of pain.
He smiled as he approached.
"Don't slip up and kill him yet!" Tiger called out. "I told you I wanted to—"
He stopped mid-sentence as he stepped into the kitchen. His eyes widened—
frozen at who he saw.
Before he could say a word, Six snapped—
"You looked in his eyes."
POW!
    "**NOOOO!**" Tiger screamed, watching as Six shot Taz in the back of the head. The bullet hit so hard it knocked Taz and the chair to the floor. Tiger stood frozen—angry, confused, eyes wide with shock.
"**WHAT THE HELL DID YOU DO?! THAT WAS MY BROTHER!**" he shouted, with tears flooding his face.
"Okay... and?" Six said coldly.
Tiger drew his pistol. In seconds, they were face to face—guns drawn,

locked in a deadly standoff.

"You killed my fuckin' brother," Tiger growled, waiting for Six to deny it—

beg to live—something.

"**NO!**" Six snapped.

"I did what you told me to do.

Tiger's hand tightened around the grip.

"You said you wanted the nigga responsible for robbin' your spot," Six added, aiming down at Taz's body. "This... is him."

Tiger wiped at the tears still pouring down. But they kept coming. His vision blurred, heart pounding, mind spinning.

The person following Taz saw Tiger go into the apartment. They'd also seen Six go in earlier and knew something was wrong. They crept inside just as Six pulled the trigger on Taz. They heard Tiger screaming and edged closer to see the aftermath.

"I'm not the enemy," Six said, walking slowly toward Tiger. He reached out, plucked the tip of Tiger's gun, and guided it down toward Taz's lifeless body.

Tiger squeezed his eyes shut, memories flashing—him and Taz as kids, the bond reignited at the burial. He knew, whatever happened, Taz was his blood—and whoever had done this was gonna pay.

"He was all I had left," Tiger said, voice tight with grief.

Six nodded. "This wasn't personal for me."

Then Six raised his gun, resting it against the back of Tiger's head. "Y'all gonna be together sooner than you—"

'**POW.**'

A shot rang out. Tiger froze, fearing he'd been hit. He turned slowly and saw Six collapse, clutching his chest.

Blood seeped, spreading fast.

Six's head swiveled toward Tiger—then toward the door. Standing there was Big Lez, tears in her eyes as she trained a .38 on Six's chest.

"I can't believe... a bitch shot me," Six gasped, breathing shallow.

"Well... at least... she fine... fuck it," he rasped, drew a final breath—and died.

Tiger stared at her, voice low:
"Why are you here?"

Lez's eyes softened. "I felt you were in trouble, so I followed you."

He shook his head. "You a terrible liar," he said with a half-smile. Then, relief hit him: "But I'm damn sure happy to see ya!"

He stepped forward and pulled her into a hug. "What about Taz?" she asked, both of them glancing back at the body.

Tiger paused. He saw a way to kill two birds. The cops were already looking for Taz and his boys as suspects. An anonymous tip would bring them running—three bodies, no questions. With Taz wanted for the murder of one of their own, the investigation would be short. As for Six? Just collateral damage. A clean exit.

He kissed Lez on the forehead as they started to head out.

"I'm more worried about how I'm gonna explain to Ice that Six is dead," Tiger said, walking toward the door.

"Who is Ice?" Lez asked.

"My connect... He gonna flip when he hear this," Tiger replied, opening her car door.

"Well, ya know I got ya back either way," she said, touching his face.

"That's cool, ma," Tiger said, knowing she had no clue how

deep this went. "But this one... I definitely gotta handle alone."

12

It Is What It Is

Tiger was at home with Cookie. It had been a couple days since the Southside massacre—where he lost his brother. He wasn't in the mood to do much of anything. He's cancelled on Lez when she asked him to come by. He even pushed back the meeting with Detective Holzendorf about finding a new connect. With DJ gone, Lez still healing, the Southside blazing from back-to-back murders, and a strong gut feeling the F.E.D.s were watching—Tiger wasn't moving many kilos. Outside of the boys out in Sherwood, he was only averaging three to five a week. Nowhere near enough to match the quality and volume he brought in monthly.

Tiger had been deep in thought. Should he start dealing with Domino... or cut his losses and get out while he still could? The game wasn't what it used to be. Now it was all murder and mayhem. Everybody gunning for the man on top. Cookie's words kept echoing—settling down, marriage, family. Could that even be real for him?

To make it worse, Tiger could feel it—he might be on the verge of losing his connect. Cookie woke Tiger up to breakfast in bed.

"How ya feeling?" she asked, concerned.

"I'm good," he responded, sitting up. She kissed his cheek and handed him the remote.

"Let's see who else done died," Tiger joked, turning on the TV. Channel9 was already on—the Southside murders, involving Taz, were live. "I'm on the Southside in Ft.Caroline Arms apartments, where behind me... just a few days ago, four people were found dead, including retired Marine Staff Sgt.Ivan Xavier—known to his platoon as Sgt.S.I.X." They flashed a picture of Six in uniform. "Also found were Champ Phillips, Larry Long, and Trevor McMillan." Photos appeared of Champ, Spank, and Taz. "Police also found a bag with over $100,000 cash, two kilos of cocaine, and two loaded 9mm pistols. Larry Long, Champ Phillips, and Trevor McMillan all suffered gunshot wounds to the back of the head, while Sgt. Six had a wound to his chest."

Tiger's eyes glued to the screen, his phone buzzed. It was Dred, one of his lieutenants from the spot on 16th and Myrtle.

"Wassup?" Tiger answered.

"You watching the news?" Dred asked, breathing hard.

"Yeah... Wzup?" Tiger replied.

"Remember we tried to explain to you 'bout who robbed us?" Dred said, circling the point.

"That's them niggas," Dred confirmed.

Tiger froze—couldn't speak. "Let me call ya back," he finally muttered, dropping the phone, shocked and hurt.

"Right under my fuckin' nose!" he snapped to himself, staring at the TV. The report continued: "If you remember, Larry Long and Trevor McMillan were wanted for questioning in the murder of Officer Shephard. JSO recently upheld a witness and video.

But now, with the recent discoveries of guns found, JSO may have a murder weapon."

"I can't believe I fell for his bullshit!" Tiger snapped. "And I was in that apartment with my money and my coke—and just left out!" He was pacing, mind racing.

His phone rang—Ice. "Here come the bullshit!" Tiger muttered, seeing the number.

"Yeah, wzup, buddy?" he answered, calm.

"You tell me!" Ice snapped. "Wzup with Six? He hasn't checked in in a few days."

Tiger slid into the truth. "Man... shit's been crazy the last couple days."

"I'm not a piece of bread, so don't try to butter me up," Ice cut him off.

"So give it to me straight."

Tiger exhaled. "Six found out who was responsible for hittin' my spot."

"Okay! And?"

"It was my brother."

"I know," Ice replied flatly.

"Hold up—so you knew about this?! And nobody bothered to tell me?" Tiger exploded.

"I told you once already—lower your damn voice when you talkin' to me!" Ice snapped, cold "Secondly, he was sent to do a job that you were apparently unable to do."

"But that was my brother!" Tiger pressed.

"Fuck that!" Ice shot back. "That's your personal life! It was business for Six."

"So nobody thought I needed to know—it was my lil brother?"

"Six said he asked you what you wanted him to do with 'em clowns, and you said 'off 'em... Not **ONCE** did you ask who they

118

were!"

"I shouldn't have to!" Tiger yelled.

"Enough of this sideways talk!" Ice snapped. "Wzup wit Six? Why haven't I heard from him?"

Tiger froze. Then he said "So you'll know...Six is dead."

A long pause, then Ice asked coolly: "Dead, huh? So how'd that happen?"

"Well, it's like this..." Tiger answered. "He killed my people— and somebody killed him."

Cookie slipped in beside him, wrapping her arm around his waist. "Are you okay?" she murmured. He nodded as Ice continued.

"So that's wzup," Ice said. "So I see you ready to step up with the big dogs, huh?

Make your own rules!

Tiger clenched his jaw. "I ain't tryin' to go there wit you, Ice— but it is what it is."

"You right...it is what it is! And how I see it, you owe me a life for a life."

"My brother was that life!" Tiger snapped.

"Nah," Ice insisted. "That was business!!!

Six was personal."

Tiger closed his eyes, fed up. "Like I said, my nigga... it is what it is."

***

Later that evening, Tiger met up with Big Lez. They sat down to go over everything she could remember from the night she was attacked. "Taz came by for me to cook him up some dope," she started. "When you pulled up, I made them leave. But after you left... he came back.

She paused, eyes distant.

119

"I thought it was you, so I answered the door wearin' what I had on when you were here."Tiger sat silent, listening. Lez was holding it together—but just barely.

"He started grabbin' me, sayin', 'You gonna gimme that pussy!' So I... I—" Her voice cracked, hands trembling.

Tiger stepped forward, wrapped her in his arms. "I gotcha, ma," he whispered, holding her tight. "If you don't wanna talk about it, it's ok, you don't have to."

"Nah, I'm good," she said after a moment, taking a deep breath. She wiped the tears from her face and straightened up.

"Where was I?" she asked.

Before Tiger could answer, she picked back up. "Oh yeah... I kneed him in the groin and ran in the room. He was right behind me."

She stopped, trying to piece it together. This was the part where everything started to blur.

"That's when I... I..." She closed her eyes, trying to pull the memory forward. "My gun was on the bed, so I ran for it. When I turned to scare him with it, he knocked it outta my hand and punched me."

Tiger's jaw tightened. He could feel the heat rising in his chest.

"He tried to climb on top of me, so I scratched at his eyes. He snatched away... then shot me."

Lez's hands moved to her stomach, and when she looked up, she locked eyes with Tiger."That's all I remember," she said quietly.

"The doctor said that you were shot twice," Tiger replied.

"I know," Lez said.

"I only remember bein' shot once."

Tiger stared at her, taking in her strength, her pain. Then he hesitated.

"Doc also said—"

"He said what?" Lez asked.

Tiger didn't answer right away.

"Don't do that," she pushed. "What did he say?"After a beat, Tiger finally spoke.

"He said... you were raped."

13

Playin' the Plug

Tiger finally decided to meet up with Domino(Det. Holzendorf) and discuss a possible connect deal. Tiger agreed to meet him at Paxon park later that evening. Tiger watched as Domino pulled next to him in a Cadillac CTS. "Wzup, my boy?" Domino stated, stepping out of his car; as he and Tiger began walking across the court to the bench for privacy.

"I'm chillin" Tiger responded. "It's a couple thangs going on right now that I had to handle, that's why I haven't got back witcha yet" Tiger explained, as he continued. "But I got a lil suttin suttin set up, But, you may not agree wit how we gotta handle the deal"

Domino gave him a sideways look as he asked, "How we gotta handle it?" he asked, mouth watering for Tiger to reveal his sources.

"Well, my people don't know ya yet, and it's a lil early to bring ya in." Tiger began slowly.

"So let me guess" Domino cut in.

"You want me to send my money, without seeing my product?"

"Pretty much" Tiger agreed. "But it aint like I'mma bring ya back some trash... This'll be some top of the line fish scale" Tiger added. Domino thought for a moment then replied, 'What's to keep you from running off with my money?" After a couple seconds of thought, Tiger replied, "Nothing!"

"Exactly!" Domino cut in, as he stood up and walked around the bench.

"So basically you saying, I have to meet you in a secluded park or something, give you my money, you leave with my money, and I wait somewhere and HOPE you come back?"

Domino began to laugh making Tiger laugh also. "I aint saying that, homie" Tiger began.

"What I'm saying is -"

Tiger paused for a moment then stated, "I guess that is what I'm saying"

"I don't know"

Domino stated, shaking his head.

"Seems I'm takin to big of a risk...

What you risking?"

"Absolutely Nothing!" Tiger snapped. "This is something you said you wanted" Tiger began. "Now if I'm wrong let me know, and we can call the whole thing off" Tiger pretended to be picking up his phone and making a call.

"Hold up a second" Domino stopped him,

as Tiger knew he would.

"Is there a safer, or more professional way

to do this?"

Tiger glanced down at his phone at a text that Cookie just sent him when he thought about this deal. So far Domino has seemed to check out. He's got his own money, Girls, swagger, and he talks street; the complete opposite

of an undercover.

Tiger finally said it: "How 'bout this," he stated, coming up with an idea. "We meet at my house this one time." Domino paused—giving Tiger room to finish. "After this, if my people still ain't ready to meet you, you gonna have to supply the spot." Domino nodded in agreement as Tiger continued.

"So it's official then," Tiger confirmed. "We meet at my house, you drop the cash, I go and handle that, you come back and get ya work—and everything's good." Domino stared at Tiger with a half-cut smile. He got what Tiger was doing—cutting out the hand-to-hand, keeping his cash off the table. All he'd risk was possession or conspiracy to deliver. With the right lawyer and Tiger's profile, he might get only three years. But Domino had a plan—he'd put Tiger away for a real long time.

"I guess that's okay," Domino replied.

"Cool!" Tiger snapped with a smile. "I'll call you sometime tomorrow...I gotta make sure he's straight," Tiger added, tossing Domino off guard so he wouldn't sense too much confidence.

Tiger was made up—this shipment was his last. Too much corruption in his own game room, and if he didn't quit now, it'd be too late. "How many you think you'll be needing?" Tiger asked as they walked back to their cars. "Depends what he charge for each one," Domino responded. Tiger knew Domino paid $28K per kilo, and figured he'd get his price. "Twenty-three," Tiger told him.

"That's a bet!" Domino said excitedly.

They gave each other dap and were about to part ways when Domino asked, "We gonna always have to do it like this? Or am I gonna eventually get to meet the connect?"

Tiger smiled. "Ya never can tell, Mr. Domino...Ya never can tell."

***

Pie Yay was at the movie theater with one of his many dime pieces when his phone lit up with a call from Heavy.

"Way ya at?" Heavy asked.

"I'm at the movies with one of my afternoon snacks... wzup?"

"You ain't forget about this evening, did ya?"

"If you talkin' 'bout your boy dem comin' in from Atlanta, then nah,

I ain't forgot," Pie Yay confirmed.

"Well, they'll be here around six, and it's one o'clock already."

"I gotcha, big homie," Pie Yay promised. "I'mma let her watch this lil movie first. Then I told her I'mma run her by Foot Locker to get the new J's... after that, I'mma run her by Mickey D's to get suttin' to eat, then it's on to the Budget Inn so I can pound on her for a while."

Both Pie and Heavy laughed.

"Just remember... six o'clock."

"I gotcha, bruh," Pie Yay responded, eyes roaming his date's big ass as they walked inside the theater. "SIX O'CLOCK, PIE!" Heavy added one last time for confirmation.

"ALRIGHT!" Pie yelled, then hung up.

"Who was that?" his date asked, as they found seats up top. Pie shot a disappointed look at her. "You promised that if I took you out, you wouldn't talk much on this date."

"Now, you wouldn't be a liar, would ya?" he joked as they settled in—only about ten

people in the theater.

As the lights dimmed and the movie started, Pie unbuttoned his pants, grabbed her hand, and slid it onto his manhood—leaning back, eyes half-closed, easing into the stroke. He never noticed the figure across the aisle, watching his every move.

By the end of the movie, he'd already been relieved—and now

he was recharged for round two. Leaving the theater, Pie Yay locked eyes with the dude who'd been watching him earlier—mean mug on full display.

He turned to his date.

"You know that dude over there?" he asked, pointing toward the spot.

They both looked—nobody there.

"What guy you talkin' 'bout?" she asked, wrapping her arms around him.

Pie knew he wasn't trippin'...

but the guy was gone.

"Don't worry 'bout it," he said, brushing off the vibe like it was just in his head.

Cruising across town with the top down on his '73 Impala, Pie Yay still hadn't noticed he was being followed. That same car tailed him to Foot Locker... and again to McDonald's. But Pie was locked in—more focused on how thick his girl was than anything else. The full date budget—including the motel—was two-sixty, and he planned on makin' her earn every penny... his way.

"You enjoyed ya'self so far?" Pie asked as they headed to the room.

"I sure have!" she said, smiling. "And thanks for the J's—I got just the outfit to rock wit them.

Pie nodded, eyeing her up and down. She caught the look and gave him one right back. Then she stepped in close, grabbed his hand, and placed it on her ass.

In a sultry tone, she whispered, "Now it's time for me to help you enjoy yaself."

***

Tiger was at home getting Domino's ten kilos together, while

Domino had his colleagues watching Tiger's every move. They were hoping he would lead them to his connect. By the time Tiger called Domino and told him he was ready, they had already reported that he hadn't been anywhere all day. That was all the confirmation Domino needed—Tiger had a stash somewhere in the house. He just needed to complete the deal, get a warrant, come back, and build a concrete case.

Tiger's phone rang—it was Ice.

Tiger had been hoping he'd call to clear everything up. Maybe call it

all a misunderstanding.

"Yeah!" Tiger answered bluntly.

"Today is the day you repay your debt to me," Ice began. "A life for a life."

Tiger became enraged and started yelling through the phone. But Ice had already hung up.

"I see now that thangs about to get reeeal stupid," Tiger stated, thinking hard about what he was gonna do about the Ice situation.

***

Pie Yay had been entertaining his date for a while now. She was stretched out across the bed, sleep. Pie Yay figured it was a better time than any to dip out.

"She's a pretty girl," Pie thought. "Somebody'll come get her."

He stepped out the hotel room and headed toward his car— unaware that the person watching him was finally about to make their move. Pulling up at the light, Pie Yay paid no attention to the car pulling up next to him. Boppin' his head back and forth to Young Jeezy, he hadn't noticed the guy beside him aiming a pistol.

Pie Yay was in the straight lane when the turn light changed, and he remembered he had something to do in that direction. Missing his opportunity, the gunman immediately followed— gun cocked and ready.

At the intersection of Commonwealth and Lane Avenue, Pie got caught by another light. Slowly, the gunman pulled up beside him again. This time, Pie glanced over. He did a double take— something about dude looked familiar.

His phone vibrated, pulling his attention.

It was Tiger. Pie turned the radio down and answered. "Wzup bruh?" he asked, glancing left to see if the mystery guy was still there.

Tiger said he was callin' to check on er'body. "Well, I'm good," Pie Yay replied, cruising through the light and pulling up to the gas station. "You aahite?"

Tiger told Pie he needed to hook up with him and Heavy later. "I'm supposed to hook up wit Fat Boy anyway, in about an hour," Pie added.

"You can get down if ya want to," he continued, sliding his credit card into the pump.

With his back turned to the road, he never saw the guy who'd been following him pull up beside his car.

After hanging up with Tiger, Pie turned and tossed his phone on the front seat—then noticed the stranger parked next to him.

He reached for his pistol—but remembered it was under the front seat.

Trying not to show any fear, he asked quickly, "Cuz, do I know you?"

The man just stood there, staring at Pie Yay—silent. Pie quickly fanned him off, turned his back, and finished pumping gas. When he glanced back, the mystery man was gone.

"Bitch ass," Pie mumbled to himself. He jumped in his car, cranked the music to capacity, and drove off.

Pulling up to the light, Pie checked his phone to see what time it was. It was 5:15 p.m. He knew he had to be heading to Heavy's if he was going to be there on time. While waiting on the light, Pie reached under his seat for his pistol. He refused to be caught slipping like he was moments ago. He could feel the tip of the gun—it had slid too far back to get a proper grip on it. *Must've slid farther back while driving*, Pie thought. As he reached deeper under the seat, the mystery man pulled up fast beside his car and jumped out—
holding a semi-automatic AR-15.

Pie glanced over but couldn't react in time. The gunman stepped to Pie Yay's door and sprayed him at point-blank range. With the top down, it wasn't hard for him to hit his target.
Pie Yay slumped over the steering wheel as his car rolled slowly into the intersection. An eighteen-wheeler hauling metal and pipe was coming through the light. Pie Yay's car crept out in front of it.
The driver laid on the horn, but it was too late. The truck slammed into the driver's side, slinging Pie about twenty yards and folding his car nearly in half.

The gunman stood there, watching the whole ordeal. He saw Pie Yay's body lying in the street in an awkward position. People started coming from all directions, rushing to help. The gunman picked up his phone and made a call.
"It's done," he said into the receiver. "Our friend is now a memory."

14

Crossed Wires, Crossed Lines

Tiger called Domino to let him know he was ready. The detective had already alerted his staff leader — warrants and backup were on standby. This was the day they brought down Operation Tiger's Den. Even without any of Tiger's affiliates locked up yet, Domino figured the threat of life in prison would make Tiger cooperate—for Cookie's sake.

He sent Cookie over to her mom's for a few hours. He didn't want her around for this; especially at the house. In the garage, he tucked Domino's bag in a hidden spot until he arrived. Domino had only handed over $200,000 of the $230,000 owed. The detective knew: taking money during a drug exchange with an undercover counts as hand-to-hand sales — and the charge gets way heavier when the buyer is also the witness. Ten kilos was enough weight to put Tiger away for a long time — and clean the streets at the same time.

Tiger was heading into the kitchen when his phone rang. It was Pie Yay — prolly reminding him about meeting with Heavy. He answered: "I got suttin' to handle real quick, then I'll be on my way."

The voice on the other end cut him off:

"You don't know me, but I found this phone... your number was the last contact."

"That's my homeboy's phone," Tiger said, uneasy. "And how you say you end up wit it?"

"It was on the ground."

"Where?" Tiger snapped.

"On the corner of Commonwealth and Lanes."Tiger's pulse spiked. He opened his mouth when the stranger dropped the shocker: "I think the guy that owned this phone... may be dead."
***

Ms. Kat was on the front porch playing with Tamela, Ace's daughter, when Tamika—Ace's baby momma—pulled up with the police behind her. Ms. Kat watched as she stepped up with a sassy look on her face.

"You have some nerve coming up to my house!" Ms. Kat snapped, mean-mugging Tamika.

"I'm not here to cause problems," she began, as the police walked up beside her.

"Well, what do you want?" Ms. Kat asked, eyeing the police. "And why are you here?"

Tamika glanced at the officer, then back at Ms. Kat with an evil smirk.

"I'm here to get my daughter."

She reached for Tamela, but Ms. Kat turned slightly away.

"This is why I brought the nice officer," Tamika added, arms out. "I didn't want a repeat of what happened at your son's funeral."

Ms. Kat looked from the officer back to Tamika and huffed, "You don't even want her!"The officer gave a sympathetic look. "I'm just here to keep the peace. But if the baby's hers, ma'am..."

He looked at Tamika. "We'll have to return her to the biological mother."

Tamika smiled and reached for Tamela again. "And the last time I checked..." Tamika smirked. "I am her biological mother."

"Since when?" Ms. Kat mumbled low, just enough for Tamika to hear.

"Since now," Tamika snapped, grabbing Tamela from her arms. "You know she's all I have left of my son—and you come here with this **SHIT!**" Ms. Kat fired off. "Ooooh, language," Tamika mocked, kissing Tamela on the cheek. "What would Jesus say?"

As Tamika and the officer turned to walk off, Tamika paused and delivered her final blow.

"I do commend Ace on one thing," she began. "He had an account and a life insurance policy for Tamela—one hunnit grand. So know that your granddaughter will be well taken care of." "It's always 'bout the money with you," Ms. Kat growled through clenched teeth.

"Well, that's no longer a problem," Tamika fired back, kissing Tamela again. "You turned out to be beneficial to me after all."

As she turned away, Ms. Kat called out,

"You gonna get everything you deserve."

Tamika stopped, smirked, and looked back.

"I really hope so, Ms. Kat... Allll one. Hundred. Thousand of it."

15

Final Play

Tiger pulled up to the house and noticed Cookie wasn't there. "She must've went back round to her mom's house," he mumbled, dialing her number again. "Answer ya phone," he huffed, sent to voicemail for the third time.

Walking inside, he figured the first thing he needed was a shower. Being with Lez, he smelled like a mix of sex, sweat, and Polo cologne. After he got clean, he planned to hit Domino to close out the deal—

then slide by Heavy's and figure out how to handle this Pie situation.

Detective Holzendorf had undercover units rolling by Tiger's spot on rotation—checking for movement, alerting when he pulled in or anything strange went down.

As soon as they confirmed Tiger was home, Holzendorf tried to call.

No answer.

"He must think this a game," the detective muttered to the officer next to him.

"Send another car by... I'mma call him one more time. And if I don't get an answer..."

He tightened his jaw. "I'm goin' in."

While Tiger was in the shower, he'd left his phone on vibrate in his pants. He couldn't hear the missed calls stacking up—two of them being from Cookie. After drying off, he grabbed the bag of marked money Domino had given him and carried it into the garage. Behind his stand-up toolbox, Tiger had a secret wall he used to stash his money. He pulled out the bag with the ten kilos, placed it on the table, and got ready to wrap the deal. He reached for his phone to hit Domino—then realized he left it in the room. Juggling too much at once, he forgot to fully conceal the cash.

Back in the garage after grabbing his phone, he saw Cookie had called. He was just about to hit her back when he heard the front door slam open.

"There she go right there," he mumbled to himself. "She sound madder than a mug."

He left everything where it was and walked toward the door with a grin—already picturing Cookie pissed... and how fun it was gonna be making up.

Tiger hid in the kitchen, planning to playfully scare Cookie when she walked past. But he froze—his grin dropped into a hard frown—when he saw the silhouette of a man with a gun. Easing back into the corner, he moved quietly, trying to make it to the garage where he might at least find a weapon. His 40 caliber was in the closet. His 9mm in the truck.

And he couldn't get to either of them.

He needed to get a better look—figure out who was in his house. All he caught was a glimpse of the man's back as he turned down the hallway. The intruder walking the opposite direction gave Tiger the break he needed.

He slipped into the garage. Moving fast through the dim light, Tiger didn't see the box of Christmas ornaments stacked near the door. "What the—" he huffed, catching his balance.

He was certain that whoever was in the house also heard it. He ducked behind a stack of bins, holding his breath as he heard footsteps coming toward the garage.

"Who the fuck is in my house?" he muttered, mind racing, trying to decide his next move.

Glancing around the garage for a weapon, Tiger noticed he'd left the duffel bag with the dope sitting on the table—and forgot to fully cover the wall where his money was stashed. "**FUUUUCK**," he hissed, grinding his teeth.

He started to move, ready to dart out and hide everything—then froze when he heard the garage door creak open slow.

"Shit, shit, shit," he lipsynced, heart thudding as the gunman stepped inside.

Tiger just hoped Cookie didn't pick this moment to come home. She'd called earlier. He never hit her back. Still squatting in the corner, helpless and tight, Tiger remembered—his phone was in his pocket. He could at least alert somebody. The closer the gunman crept, the clearer his face became.

Tiger watched him walk straight to the table with the duffel. Watched him unzip it. The man glanced around real quick—like he expected someone to run up on him—then zipped it shut again. Tiger thought he'd grab the bag and bounce. But no... he wasn't done. He was still lookin'—searchin' for something else. That's when it clicked. This wasn't a robbery.

This was a hit.

Ice had a nigga follow me to the house, he thought. *So he gonna play me like that, huh? That's wzup!*

Tiger had his phone out, about to text Heavy and have him

rush over with some artillery, when he saw the gunman moving closer in his direction.

Tiger's face twisted, rage rising, when he finally got a clear view.

Domino! he mumbled under his breath.

He tried to piece together the link between Domino and Ice. He'd met Domino way before the fallout with Ice ever happened. Was meeting you really a coincidence? Or were you sent, you bastard? Tiger's jaw locked as he watched Domino fumbling through boxes. *Why you ain't take the dope and leave?* Tiger thought

The answer hit like a punch to the gut. Domino walked back over to the duffel, pulled out his chirp phone, and said, "This is Detective Holzendorf... the house is clear."

Tiger's eyes flew open, heat rushing to his face. "I've confiscated the ten kilos of cocaine from inside the garage," Domino continued, looking around. "There's no sign of the money, or the perp, at this time."

"This nigga been setting me up the whole time", Tiger muttered, shifting deeper into the corner. He could feel time running out. Cops would be swarming the spot any minute. He needed to disappear—and fast.

And Cookie.

He had to warn her.

He was sure they had something on her too, and he refused to let her get caught in this.

He'd go down before he let her

get hit with conspiracy.

Detective Holzendorf moved toward the door leading into Tiger's house. For a moment, it looked like Tiger might actually have an escape route. But just before the detective opened the door, he turned to scan the garage one last time. That's when he saw it—a mirror hanging in the corner. Looking into it, he spotted a flicker of movement behind some stacked boxes near the side door.

"**Tiger**," he mumbled with a slow grin.

He stepped away from the door casually, trying not to startle Tiger or tip him off that he'd been made. He kept his eyes flicking to the mirror, using it like a rearview as he crept closer. Tiger clocked the way he was moving—too careful, too slow. Something was off.

Then he spotted it.

The mirror.

His reflection.

Shit. He had to move. Now.

Without hesitation, Tiger bolted from behind the boxes and lunged for the side door. As he pushed it open, Det. Holzendorf raised his pistol and shouted, "**FREEZE!**"

He crept up behind him.

"**DON'T MOVE! I MEAN IT! DON'T... MOVE!**"

Phone in one hand, gun in the other, he called for backup. But Tiger wasn't just standing there—he was watching him through the same mirror. And the moment that gun dipped an inch too low—

Tiger took off.

"**HE'S ON THE RUN!**" Holzendorf roared, chasing him into the backyard.

"**HE'S HEADING FOR THE FENCE!**"

Tiger cleared the fence without even touching it. "**HE'S ACROSS THE FENCE!**" the detective barked, scrambling after him.

Tiger cut through one yard, crossed the street, hit another. He was moving. Fast.

"I SEE HIM!" Holzendorf yelled, losing ground. Tiger's lead stretched further with every stride. Holzendorf knew if backup didn't box him in soon, he'd vanish.

"I WANT TWO CARS ON EVERY CORNER FOR TEN BLOCKS!" he shouted, watching Tiger leap fences like hurdles.

"This son of a bitch is not getting away!"

He raised his gun again.

"I SAID FREEEEZE!"

Tiger didn't stop. Not for nothing.

Holzendorf took the shot.

The bullet slammed into a tree inches from Tiger's shoulder.

"DAMN IT!"

He snatched up the chirp again.

"WHERE'S MY HELICOPTER? WHERE ARE THE CARS I ASKED FOR? GET! ME! Tiger!"

Tiger kept moving—hopping fences, weaving through cut-throughs, turning the neighborhood into his escape route. He knew this part of the city like the back of his hand and he used it to his advantage.

Cop sirens howled up and down the blocks. A helicopter hovered overhead, its spotlight sweeping the dark.

Tiger crouched low in a patch of thick bushes, yanked out his phone, and called Heavy. He needed an exit. Fast.

They agreed to meet at the football field.

But with every street crawling with cops, Heavy couldn't come to him. If Tiger wanted out—really out—he'd have to go back through the heart of the danger.

Seeing the coast was clear, Tiger stepped out the bushes and made his way toward the park. He needed to cross Fifth Street to get back to the back roads. Just as he hit the street, headlights lit up behind him. He didn't wait—he sprinted toward the nearest yard with a fence.

"**STOP!**" a voice shouted behind him.

"**Tiger!**"

He turned, recognizing the voice.

Cookie?

She was already out the car,

running toward him.

"You can't be out here right now, baby... it's not safe," he said, breath short.

"Come get in the car," Cookie said. "You gotta get out the neighborhood."

He spotted her car still running, door wide open in the road.

"I can't go with you!" he said, eyes darting. "They got the whole neighborhood surrounded." That's when he saw it. A gray Grand Marquis hook-slide onto Fifth Street—

right toward her car.

"You gotta go!" he yelled, while taking off running again.

But when he looked back—Cookie was right behind him. And jumping out that Grand Marquis, not far off, was Detective Holzendorf. Tiger made a hard turn toward a backyard he knew had a hole in the fence that led straight into the park.

"**FREEEEZE!** Tiger, stop!" Holzendorf shouted, falling farther behind.

Tiger shot through the opening and kept going. "Baaaby... help me!" Cookie cried, her shirt was caught in the fence.

Tiger skidded to a stop—hesitated—then shot back for her.

Her being stuck gave Holzendorf a chance to gain some ground. He was just a few feet from Cookie by the time Tiger freed her. Holzendorf tried rushing through the fence the same way but got caught up.

"**STOP! DAMNIT, STOP!**" he yelled, wrestling with the fence.

Tiger grabbed Cookie's hand and yanked her along. She was slowing him down, no doubt—but he refused to leave her.

They were just steps away from Ms. Davis's yard—the one that led into the park—when Holzendorf shouted out, "**TIGERRR!**"

Then the gunshot rang out.

Tiger kept running. Then he felt Cookie's hand rip away from his.

He turned. She was falling.

His eyes widened.

"Baby, come on!" he said, panicked.

From the look on her face, he knew—.

she was hit.

He ran back and dropped to his knees, pulling her into his arms. She was lying on her back, eyes wet. He looked over his shoulder—Holzendorf was still tangled in the damn fence. Cookie's breathing got heavy, and Tiger was scrambling in his mind. He didn't know what to say, what to do. He felt moisture under her back—looked at his hand.

Blood.

His whole body locked up.

He rocked her back and forth. "It'll be okay," he kept saying.

He couldn't promise her that.

He didn't even believe it himself. But he needed to say it.

He glanced around for help, even though he knew damn well there wasn't none coming for him.

"Hang in there, baby," he mumbled, sirens wailing in the distance.

Cookie looked up at him, her lip trembling.

"I... I'm sorry."

"What, baby?" Tiger asked,

grateful she was still speaking.

140

She was gasping now,

trying to get more words out.

"Ssshh," Tiger whispered, signing her to be still. This felt like the end.

And if it was—he'd trade his life to save hers.

"I love you, baby," Tiger said, with his voice cracking. "I'm so sorry for exposing you to this way of life."

Cookie smiled, hearing him say love. He never said that. Usually it was just One Love.

If this was how she had to go—this moment, in his arms—it couldn't be more perfect.

"I love you," Cookie whispered back.

Her breaths got heavier as Tiger panicked."**SOMEBODY HEEELP!**" he screamed, looking around frantically.

Cookie slowly reached up, her hand brushing Tiger's face.

"**I'm here, baby,**" he said, teary-eyed.

"**Kiss me,**" she whispered—

smiling through the tears.

Tiger leaned in and kissed her—deeper than he ever had in his life.

When he pulled back, their eyes locked.

Then her hand went limp.

Her head dropped to the side.

She wasn't breathing.

"Baby! **BABY!**" Tiger yelled, voice cracking as panic took over. "**NOOOO!**"

That's when Det. Holzendorf finally made it through the fence.

Tiger eased Cookie's body down onto the street. There was no reason to stick around now. She'd given her life for him to be free—he wasn't about to let that be in vain.

"Don't move!" Holzendorf shouted, running toward him.

Tiger took one last look at Cookie, then bolted—cutting across to Ms. Davis's yard.

There was an eight-foot concrete wall standing between him and freedom.

Holzendorf knew he wouldn't catch him in time, so he stopped, raised his gun, and shouted— "**TIIIGGGEEERRR!**"

Tiger stopped about ten yards from the wall and turned to face him. The detective crept closer, pistol drawn. Tiger was tired—but angrier than anything. He had to get this shit off his chest.

"It's over," Holzendorf said, glancing down at Cookie's body.

Tiger shook his head. "You really had me going there for a minute... Domino—I mean, *Detective* Holzendorf, is it?"

"Yeah, well... just doing my job," the detective replied, inching closer.

"Your job, huh? Was she a part of your damn job?" Tiger snapped, pointing at Cookie.

"She was an accident. You know it,"

Holzendorf pleaded.

"Explain that to her," Tiger growled, grinding his teeth.

"It's over, Tiger. You got nowhere to go," Holzendorf said, trying to stay calm.

"Why don't you just turn around and put your hands on your head?"

"I got plenty of places to go," Tiger mumbled, turning his back. "And jail ain't one of 'em."

He glanced over his shoulder—Holzendorf was kneeling beside Cookie, calling for paramedics. Ten yards.

An eight-foot fence.

That's all that stood between Tiger and freedom. No hesitation.

Tiger took off.

"Hey! **HEY!**" Holzendorf yelled. "**STOP!** Damnit, stop or I'll shoot!"

Tiger didn't break stride.

One leap—he hit the top of the fence.

Holzendorf took aim. As Tiger went over...

POW.

16

The Trial

Three months had passed since Operation Tiger's Den was dismantled. Detective Holzendorf and his team had confiscated ten kilos of cocaine, an unregistered .40 caliber pistol, and two hundred thousand dollars in marked money from inside the house. Before Tiger's truck got hauled off to impound, they found another twenty kilos in a hidden floor compartment—along with an unregistered 9mm pistol. Holzendorf built his entire case around Tiger's link to DJ and the fact that Tiger used his home as a stash house.

The charges were stacked: possession of a controlled substance equal to or exceeding 10,000 grams; constructive and actual possession of a firearm by a convicted felon; racketeering; possession of a controlled substance with intent to sell; and conspiracy to possess a controlled substance with intent to distribute. Any one of those charges could land a life sentence.

Holzendorf took the stand, testifying to every piece of evidence he'd gathered—photos from DJ's apartment, the conversation he recorded with Tiger about the drugs, the whole setup. But the defense team came swinging. They ripped into two key flaws:

One—Tiger had never been caught selling or physically holding any of the evidence listed. Two—and this was the kicker—Tiger wasn't even the one on trial.

Cookie was.

Miraculously, Cookie survived being shot in the back—despite two weeks in intensive care under federal supervision. Tiger was never caught. He'd escaped, lucky as hell, even with all the commotion. Detective Holzendorf, frustrated and empty-handed, made his move: if they couldn't get Tiger, they'd charge Cookie. He'd seen that look in Tiger's eye the night of the shooting—dude was ready to give himself up if it meant saving her.

Three months passed. Still no sign of Tiger.

Heavy pulled one of the best defense attorneys he could find to represent Cookie. She sat in the courtroom now, silent, waiting for the jury to return from deliberation. Every so often, she looked back over her shoulder—hoping, praying, that Tiger would show. Holzendorf did the same. Deep down, she knew it was unlikely... but that hope? That's what kept her breathing.

An hour later, the jury filed back in. You could see it on Cookie's face—panic rising, stomach tight—as the judge read the verdict, then passed it to the jury foreman.

Her lawyer had gone to war for her—built a strong case around lack of evidence, hearsay, and straight-up slander. But Cookie had a gut feeling the Feds were just using her as bait. Tiger was M.I.A. She wasn't cooperating. So they came for the next best thing. She hoped they'd go lighter—seeing she wasn't the one the case was built around. Still, since she'd been out on bond, she hadn't heard a word from Tiger. Not a damn word.

She thought, *At least he coulda hit me up... see if I'm good.*
Now it was time.

Cookie and her attorney stood. The room went still.

Everyone held their breath as the first of five charges was read off.

As for *case #155693*, The State of Florida vs. Serena Loveless. In the charge of possession of a controlled substance, equal to or greater than 10,000 grams. We find the defendant—

There was complete silence throughout the courtroom as the foreman read off:

"**Not Guilty.**"

People in the audience applauded—loudly—even those who didn't know Cookie.

"Order!" the judge barked, banging his gavel. "Order in the court. Try to hold

back your responses until the reading of the final deliberation."

The foreman continued.

"As for the charge of possession of a controlled substance with the intent to sell..."

Cookie clasped her hands together like a prayer. "We find the defendant—**Not Guilty.**"

She smiled wide as hell, ear to ear.

Charge after charge, the verdicts came back clean. And the firearm charge? Dropped.

There was only one left standing between Cookie and her freedom—but it was the monster. The heavy one.

Everyone held their breath.

"As for the charge of conspiracy to the possession of a controlled substance with the intent to sell..."

Cookie closed her eyes.

Heavy dropped his head.

Her lawyer crossed his fingers.

The foreman read: "**Guilty.**"

Silence sliced through the courtroom sharp enough to cut steel.

Cookie blinked fast, trying to hold back the flood. A guilty verdict meant time—real time. She turned back to the audience. Found Heavy. Their eyes locked. He saw her breaking. Quietly, he raised his chin with one finger—Keep your head up.

She nodded, forcing a thin smile behind her pain. Of everyone tied to Tiger, she connected to Heavy most—he was loyal. Real. Like family. Cookie turned back as the judge leaned forward."Ms. Loveless, you have been found guilty by a jury of your peers."

Cookie glanced over at the jury—four men, two women. All of them looked over forty. *Jury of my peers, my ass*, Cookie thought as the judge continued.

He asked the routine: Did she understand what was going on? Was she competent? Did she feel her lawyer had represented her properly?

Cookie nodded. "Yes."

Didn't matter that the verdict was guilty. She wasn't about to fall apart in front of them."Sentencing will be in three weeks," the judge said.

Cookie leaned toward her lawyer, whispered something. He shook his head, tried to talk her out of it. She didn't budge.

He sighed and stood up slowly.

Seeing the movement, the judge raised an eyebrow. "Counsel, is there a problem?"

Cookie's attorney looked at her one more time—hoping she'd change her mind. She gave him a slight nudge.

He took a deep breath.

"Yes, Your Honor," he began, eyes still on Cookie. "Ms. Loveless

has decided that..."
He paused again. Another push from Cookie.
He straightened.
"Ms. Loveless has decided that, upon hearing a guilty verdict, she would like to be sentenced immediately—rather than wait the given three weeks."
Heavy sat up, surprised—but not confused. He understood. Cookie wasn't trying to drag this out. She knew it wasn't gonna make anything better with Tiger. She wanted it over with. Quick and clean. And since this was her first offense, maybe—just maybe—the judge would show some mercy.
She hoped.

The judge read through the long sheet—her rights, or lack thereof. He reminded her the charge carried a maximum of ten years to life. Cookie left it all in God's hands. Taking this charge meant Tiger wouldn't have to.
Everyone waited.
"Ms. Loveless," the judge said finally, "the court finds you guilty of conspiracy to possession of a controlled substance with the intent to sell..."
A pause. Then the drop.
"I sentence you to eight years in the women's correctional facility, with parole eligibility after thirty-six months."
He banged the gavel.
Cookie blinked—and a tear fell before she could stop it.
The guard stepped up beside her. She didn't fight. Didn't speak. Just walked—.
out the courtroom.

She took one last look at Heavy, and under her sad look he saw her soldier smile. Heavy again pointed at Cookie, then pushed his chin up. Cookie nodded, took a deep breath, and with a half cut smile, she left the courtroom with her head held high. Heavy headed out the courtroom feeling upset and proud at the same time. Standing at the elevator, he pulled out his phone and made a call. Stepping inside the elevator, he turned then stated, "The judge gave her three years on a eight" Heavy smiled with the thought of his next statement. "I gotta give it to ya" he began, then continued,

"You got a real Ride or Die Chick"

THE END